The Executioner's Tale

Guy SL.

THE EXECUTIONER'S TALE

Ginny Stroud

Matador
9 Priory Business Park,
Wistow Road, Kibworth Beauchamp,
Leicestershire. LE8 0RX
Tel: (+44) 116 279 2299
Fax: (+44) 116 279 2277
Email: books@troubador.co.uk
Web: www.troubador.co.uk/matador

ISBN 978 1783065 912

British Library Cataloguing in Publication Data.
A catalogue record for this book is available from the British Library.

Typeset by Troubador Publishing Ltd, Leicester, UK
Printed and bound by CPI Group (UK) Ltd, Croydon, CR0 4YY

Matador is an imprint of Troubador Publishing Ltd

MIX
Paper from
responsible sources
FSC® C013604

With thanks to my neighbour and Partner in crime Joan Taylor

Chapter One

THE PENSIONER'S TALE

Murder.

I believe most people have considered murder at one time or other in their lives. Who has never stated in a moment of anger "I could kill her/him". Some actually go so far as imagining the act, which is usually enough to vent their pent up frustration. A very few put their fantasies into action. An accident made me one of that number.

I'm not a monster, well I don't think I am, but probably neither do most serial killers. I am someone who crossed a line and chose not to step back. When I look in the mirror I see the same recognisable features: no horns or tail, not even a sinister glint in the eyes, just me. Okay an older, tired version but no hint of evil or madness. Perhaps that's just what Jack the Ripper saw in his reflection.

Sometimes I catch a glimpse of how others now see me. A sixty plus woman fighting the effects of gravity. Losing the battle in telltale areas around the eyes and jowls, which used to be a trim chin. A bathroom cabinet is bad enough, but I tend to avoid full length reflection: it reminds me too much of a hall of mirrors at the fun fair. Not much amusement in seeing yourself distorted into a matronly figure resembling your own grandmother. Without this reminder I feel remarkably like the self I have always known. Yes the stairs seem to have become longer and steeper, but while my joints creak in protest, I don't yet need motorised assistance up the wooden hill to Bedfordshire.

Nevertheless the wrinkles and creases betray me and reflect how the government sees me: a pensioner, OAP, senior citizen, "coffin dodger". A stereotyped member of a group who have outlived their usefulness, and then added insult to injury by surviving to claim their dues.

All years of servitude and service are conveniently forgotten. The rightful reimbursement of our financial contributions are regarded, at best, as an inconvenience, at worst as charity. We have changed in one birthday from a valuable member of society, to a drain on the very resources we provided for decades.

Yet, I have discovered that this very anonymity – being invisible – has its advantages. In this tendency to typecast the elderly, our individualism is concealed. The support stockings and high waisted trousers hide the former spy and ex commando. Generations who have faced choices and dangers most of their ancestors will thankfully never have to contemplate.

Their lives were so different – more selfless, an emphasis on family and community rather than individual desire. Their role models were their own folk not the plastic, and often amoral, media celebrities. Their values were different – a deep belief in decency and justice.

My own retirement coincided with a crisis of this

philosophy. Perhaps I had more time to see that the society around me had grown to ridicule those principles. Civilisation for all its opportunities had done the unthinkable – flushed away the baby with the bathwater.

There is an old Basuto proverb which deserves recall "If a man does away with his traditional way of living and throws away his good customs, he had better first make certain that he has something of value to replace them."

Chapter Two

THE WIFE'S TALE

Derek Jones was a truly monstrous creature, without any redeeming qualities.

He was a drunk and bully. He spent his existence between a comatose alcoholic stupor. and terrorising his brow, frequently bodily, beaten, wife. The malicious pleasure he took in this latter occupation left no room for arguments to justify this sadistic behaviour.

Unlike so many bullies, however, he did not fool his other acquaintances with outward signs of a more pleasant nature. Even his local pub landlord could barely manage a smile while supplying his daily fix. In fact the benefit of his substantial contribution to the brewery income was becoming seriously outweighed by the adverse effect on other customers.

Personally I chose to steer well clear of this individual, although I did visit his wife during his frequent absences. He could not hold down a job, so these absences were either alcohol induced or his excursions to the pub.

I liked Mary very much, so over tea and biscuits made every attempt to persuade her to leave him and/or contact the police. We became close friends: she had no one else. She did not work and had few acquaintances, let alone friends. Her husband discouraged visitors and limited her movements outside the home, thereby ensuring her isolation. Her parents were both dead; having made the prophetic forecast that if she married him she would come to regret it. She had no siblings or any other relatives, except those which might crawl from the woodwork in the event of a legacy. So for her husband it was an easy "divide and conquer" campaign.

The "couple" also had no children, and it was in the latter phase of our relationship that she confided her sad history.

The abuse began soon after their marriage and took the tragic but inevitable scenario where slaps graduated to punches and kicks. More frequently, for the sake of variety, he would employ domestic utensils as implements for punishment.

During the honeymoon period these episodes brought the usual rational moments of regret and promise. But as his sobriety deteriorated and she became thoroughly subservient these apologies changed to accusations. The "you brought this on yourself by annoying me" stage of domestic torture.

This poisonous bond was already in a well established routine by the second year of their marriage. Somehow the inevitable had so far been postponed, but, just before Christmas, Mary learned she was pregnant. The realisation brought extreme emotions: fear which was now a perpetual companion, but the faint hope that this blessing could heal their relationship.

In this desire she still badly overestimated her husband:

he was incapable of love, even to his own creation. The good news, when she nervously imparted it, resulted in a beating so severe, that not only the baby, but her potential for future child bearing was lost.

She spent that Christmas in hospital, where the irony of the nativity could not have been more painful. Luckily her spouse was celebrating the festive season too thoroughly to join the visitors for the few inpatients. The nursing staff did their best to lift her depression, and persuade her to leave the cause, without success. She remained fiercely loyal, if not to her tormentor, then to the sacred vows she took in church. So much so I think she saw this confession as a betrayal of trust and became a little uncomfortable, perhaps embarrassed, in my presence.

But this display of vulnerability meant that it was impossible to desert her and I continued, even increased, my visits. To be absolutely truthful, I was frightened that the situation would end in further heartbreak. It was no consolation to be proved correct.

One morning I called and found her lying on the kitchen floor. She was sporting the habitual swollen, cut lip and black eye, but there was something more, and after getting her upright I 'phoned the ambulance. The pain she could not disguise from the effort and her laboured breathing made me suspect fractured ribs.

Finally all pleas were heard. Enough was enough, and although she refused official help; when the time came, she discharged herself from hospital and vanished. Ironically at her weakest physical moment, she suddenly found the strength to leave and the sense to disappear without trace.

Most people now were even more wary of him: having

lost his regular punch bag they did not wish to provide a substitute. He was a large man in every bodily sense of the word and made the most of his physical dominance to intimidate all around him. But I had been in this world long enough to have encountered bullies before: in my experience bullying and cowardice walk hand in hand.

In any case I am too old and awkward to care much about public opinion let alone the likes of Mr Jones. Some grain of common sense must have remained in his pickled brain because he chose not to tangle with his ageing 5' 2" neighbour. That is until the end of November. Both our lives changed forever – in fact his ended.

That autumn day began with a note slipped through my letterbox which accused me of an anonymous complaint to the police citing domestic abuse. Someone had at last found the courage to take some action, even if was a pathetic attempt. It was not me – he should have known better. That was his first mistake.

Maybe it was an error for me to go around his door on that rainy Monday morning, but, as I say, he should have known me better. I'll admit I was annoyed at the injustice of being unfairly accused. It is a failing but such things fester in me. I was actually relieved when he opened the door and invited me inside. That was his second mistake.

The hallway led straight into the kitchen, and it looked as though he was actually sober enough, or had enough self preservation, to be trying to prepare a meal. So I hoped he would be sensible enough to be convinced I was not the author of the letter. As I began my rehearsed appeal he turned back to the table, picked up the carving knife and commenced hacking at some innocent carrots.

Even with this evident show of aggression I was not phased, although I was in no doubt that the carrots were a substitute for a more worthy but less accessible target.

As I spoke to him, he spun around, but foolishly continued chopping the hapless veggies. A hangover is not the best condition to undertake much activity and sensitive work with a sharp implement is not one of them. The first blow missed the carrots completely, but instead sliced off most of the fingers on his left hand.

It is said that where there is no sense there is no feeling, but in this instance I was wrong about Jones' intelligence because he certainly felt the loss of his digits. He jumped back towards me howling in either shock or agony. Since he was still clutching the carving knife I wisely sidestepped the oncoming lump of humanity. In doing so I nearly slipped on the collection of assorted beer and spirit bottles decorating the dirty, sticky kitchen floor. Unfortunately the amputee was not so lucky. He tripped over a vodka bottle with one foot, skated on a lager bottle with the other: slid a few feet and crashed head first into the stove.

All was silence. Now I was in a state of shock and time seemed to slow down. For seconds, which seemed like minutes, I just stared mesmorised at the bulk now lying at my feet: the blood from head and hand adding further mess to the old lino.

Even when I regained some sensation I just stared at the copse. Somehow I just knew life was extinct, but I had to check. Was it with any intention of resuscitation – if so why did I put a cloth between my fingers and his carotid pulse? There was no movement, no evidence of life. I was standing in the room with a dead man, and how did I feel. Well, honestly not very much and that shocked me more than death. I had been brought up a Christian, so why did I feel no sadness, no remorse. After all although I hadn't even touched the man it was my presence which caused his demise.

Yet the answer was there. I had grown cynical about human nature and its sanctity. I used to believe in innate human goodness and some divine justice, but saw precious little in recent years. At the very time I should have had a strong faith to cling to, increasing age was the very time I lost that conviction. Betrayal was probably the strongest emotion I now felt about man, society and God.

Then a thought came back to me from my Open University days, an idea called utilitarianism: the greater good principle. The idea that this could even be extended to humanity seemed bizarre, even humorous, at the time. Now I had to ask myself: was the once human being at my feet a greater good alive or dead .

So I made the decision and left him.

There was no evidence of my presence and even if some forensic trace remained, I had been a regular caller on his wife. My only real concern was the possibility of a witness to my visit. Even then, I reasoned, he could have been alive when I left. The day was bleak and sodden. I was suitably bundled up against the elements, in fact a regular hoodie. Moreover it was a weekday when our younger neighbours were absent in their offices and shops. However, as an extra precaution, I returned home on a circular route.

So I went home, made myself a cup of tea – amazed at my perfectly steady hands – and waited.

Chapter Three

A CHRISTMAS TALE

I waited as the week passed. I seemed to hold my breath as a week stretched into a month and time hurried towards Christmas.

It was easy most of the time to dismiss the reality of what had happened. Except as the days grew dark in the afternoons, and the nights lengthened, I thought of the corpse rotting just yards away. Sometimes I almost felt sorry for the person who had inhabited that shell and how little he was missed. I say 'almost' because it was never far from my thoughts that it could so easily have been his wife lying there.

I also realised, when I recalled events – like a student pointlessly dissecting an exam – that I had made at least one mistake. When I left the house I had dropped the lock. Oh I had not made the elementary error of leaving fingerprints for any budding CSI to discover. However in my haste to fasten the door between myself and my "crime" I had effectively sealed the house, guaranteeing a delayed discovery.

As Christmas cards were despatched, with still no detection, I was sorely tempted to break with my principles and send my own anonymous note. I was still contemplating my best course of action, when an inquisitive postman solved my dilemma. Despite the cold temperatures I imagine decomposition had reached a critical point. So raising the letterbox flap raised some suspicions: probably as well as his last meal. Finally I did feel some guilt: as I watched the police and medics enter the house to deal with the mess I had left.

In the days and weeks that followed I waited again: this time for the expected official visit. In preparation I went over the story I had rehearsed for weeks. In the meantime I kept abreast of events through every source I could without raising suspicions: neighbours, friends, the media.

Eventually the case was closed as "accident by misadventure". by which time most people were already thoroughly bored with the topic. The truth was no-one cared. It was stale news, fit for only wrapping fish and chips before health and safety intervened. No one missed, certainly not, grieved, the deceased. Even his final bodily departure would have been attended only by the undertakers and crematorium staff except for one event.

This unexpected, but, I should have known, predictable, occurrence was the return of Mary from her voluntary exile. The old friend who arrived at my door was happily a completely changed individual. Whether it was my imagination or not her facial worry lines had cleared and her shoulders no longer sagged, like the weight of the world had lifted. But most noticeable of all were her eyes. The soft brown orbs were clear and at peace: they no longer blinked in fearful anticipation. They say that the eyes are the windows to the soul: there was now no fear there.

She chose to stay at the "family" home until after the cremation. I hoped that no earth bound phantom would bother her as he had in life. I doubted it, since I, his nemesis, had experienced no vengeful apparition. In fact, since the incident, I had been blessed with reviving dreamless sleep. Could I possibly describe it as the sleep of the just?

So it was that on a cold, but dry and sunny winter day, I accompanied Mary to say our final goodbyes. Loyal to the end, she was probably his only genuine mourner. In my own case; well, like his death, my motives were for her rather than him: I would not see her grieve alone. It is a common belief that perpetrators will attend their prey's funeral. There was no sense of satisfaction, or accomplishment: just relief to see the back of him and confirm he was gone.

As his coffin slid behind the curtains en route to the furnace I felt a shocking sense of irony. I guiltily hoped that this burning of his body was a foretaste of his spiritual punishment. If I thought about religion it was not the gentle, all forgiving, New Testament teaching, but the earlier Hell and damnation variety. An "eye for an eye" judgement. The manner of his death fitted this perfectly. Two factors governed his life and literally led to his downfall: bullying and booze. If he had not turned his anger on me and then tripped on his discarded bottles, we would not be standing in this chapel watching him roll into eternity.

There was no wake: just a cup of tea and biscuits back in her kitchen. It was the first time I had returned since the accident, but I still could not summon remorse. Every time I looked at Mary it reinforced my conviction. She was alive, happy and now safe.

She left a a week later. There was nothing here for her,

but painful memories. The house, her parents' bequest, was to be sold off to pay various loan companies: the price of her husband's addiction. But, thanks to a forgotten insurance policy she would have enough a begin a new comfortable future. Derek Jones, by his death, had unwittingly provided her with the very thing he denied her in life – freedom. Like Belshazzar, the king of Babylon, he had been weighed and found wanting. He was, indeed, more valuable and useful dead than alive.

I have never considered myself a serial killer: I have never kept trophies. I get no pleasure or power from watching life depart, and would rather forget my "victims" – let alone attend their funerals. My fulfilment comes from their survivors. So maybe I do keep trophies, if so the peace I now saw in Mary's eyes was my first.

Chapter Four

THE NURSE'S TALE

Christmas and New Year came and went, followed by the usual seemingly endless months of January, February and March. This year though the winter season spread into April. It was a late Easter which finally saw a permanent change in the weather towards the middle of that month.

All was quiet, and my dubious activities may have ended there, except when spring finally came around I took advantage of the recent sunshine to visit an aunt in the north.

I can honestly say that I have never looked for targets. Candidates have always come to me. Statistics quote that in Britain you are *never* more than 20 feet away from a *rat*. In my experience I would claim you are even closer to two legged vermin.

A sad, but true, comment on modern society, which should have progressed beyond the cruelty of earlier centuries. It is a depressing observation, but human nature, unlike lesser species does have a tendency towards greed. This avarice is more often directed to money, but occasionally it includes power: then it becomes something more dangerous. True, there are wonderful people who buck the sermon of 'self' preached in the 1980s, but successive governments have been reluctant, or unable, to reverse this trend. Fighting the system has made me exhausted and disillusioned: like a salmon trying to leap Niagara. But I also feel furious for all those who voicelessly suffer, and feel like strangers in a hostile land.

Time to step off the soapbox, and head north on the M1. I only learnt to drive in my early thirties, and have never lost the pleasure of liberation it gave me. The old motorway was astonishingly free of roadworks and accidents, so I made good time reaching the Yorkshire borders in time for lunch.

My elderly aunt was waiting for me and had made a "mash". A curious northern expression, which on earlier visits caused some confusion: until it was explained that this related to tea rather than potatoes. So it was over a cup of tea and homemade cakes that I stretched out and heard the details of my next 'endeavour'.

Aunt Dot was approaching her eightieth birthday, but was doubly blessed, in that both her mind and body were sound. This lucky genetic fact enabled her to remain at home and independent. Indeed she was even able to help less fortunate neighbours. It was one of these friends who now concerned her and dominated the conversation.

It seemed that the lady, Gladys, although a contemporary of my aunt, was in a poor state, having recently suffered a stroke. She had recovered sufficiently to have returned home, a few yards around the corner from where we sat. The attack, however, had permanently removed some of her mobility and speech. So, although she could manage basic skills, she needed, and was provided a daily carer.

Since the arrival of this woman there had been a

noticeable deterioration in her friend, beyond that caused by her physical ailments. Although Gladys seemed generally more frail and nervous this was more evident on those occasions when Margaret Norris, the aforementioned carer, was present. My aunt's suspicions were aroused and she took to visiting her friend at odd hours during the day and early evening. She had done so in any case to offer assistance and companionship, but now she had a more ominous motive. Either to catch the carer in some compromising act, or persuade her friend to confide her problems. So far she had been unsuccessful in both aims.

My visit could not have been more fortuitous since my aunt wanted the opinion and advice of an independent observer. If she had knowledge of my activities during the last few months she may not have considered me so trustworthy a judge.

Aunt Dot didn't want to waste more time, so she asked if I minded accompanying her that afternoon. The visit was planned after the carer had left, so at 4pm, on the dot, we walked the short distance to Gladys' home.

As it transpired the carer had extended her visit, and I had the opportunity to assess this individual firsthand. She seemed friendly enough, perhaps too much so for my reserved southern tastes. But there was something about implied ownership of her charge which was both patronizing and menacing. Maggie Norris was amply able to do this: she was a large woman, in every sense of the word. Age: I would estimate late thirties, but there was a craggy look about her face which added a good decade. By the nature of her profession she was also physically powerful. As she stood over the seated Gladys, she talked at her without waiting for, or even expecting, a response. It resembled the relationship between a domineering parent and abused child, not that of equals.

Poor Gladys, for her part, looked humiliated, and there was desperation in the look she risked glancing at us. But when Norris bid her goodbyes with the 'threat' to return tomorrow, there was something in her eyes I had seen before – fear.

The departure of the "carer" did not release the tension: I had witnessed similar behaviour during my visits to Mary. This signified a measure of control and coercion well established and, more worrying, practised. It spoke of a someone who was used to this method of intimidation. The manipulation of weak vulnerable people: an experienced bully.

As soon as we returned home, while my aunt was still taking off her coat, she asked "did you see the marks on her arms?" I had indeed, dark bluish yellow bruises suspiciously like the shape of fingers: as if she had been grabbed or held roughly. Telltale evidence pointing, at best to careless neglect, at worst deliberate maltreatment. Later, over yet another "mash" Aunt Dot confided a further cause for concern – as if physical abuse wasn't enough. It seemed that certain valuable items had mysteriously disappeared. I was hardly surprised: but the combination of theft with brutality meant we were dealing with an extremely sadistic and calculating individual.

The missing items were mainly small but precious trinkets. Gold and silver jewellery which once adorned their owner's neck and hands. Wedgewood and Royal Doulton pottery which had held pride of place on her mantelpiece.

When quizzed about their whereabouts Gladys seemed vague and nervous. But the most damning thing was the unaccountable loss of her wedding ring. The only thing she retained from an early marriage, which ended some sixty years ago on a forgotten Korean battlefield.

My aunt and I discussed options: which ranged from confrontation to more furtive means. Retirement does have a few advantages, one of them being the liberty of time. I now planned to extend my original one week's visit for as long as necessary. I was worried for my aunt: a combination of her suspicions and guileless nature might well put her in the firing line. My more cynical view of humanity convinced me we were dealing with a ruthless, serial criminal. Certainly her unprincipled behaviour in the ill treatment of her vulnerable client testified to that. But I was concerned how far her self preservation could take her. If I had known then how far the slippery slope had already taken Maggie Norris I would have been scared to death.

Fortunately we were oblivious to the real situation as we discussed our strategy. Of course my law abiding aunt was all for contacting the authorities in the shape of the private home care firm or the police. For my part I was not convinced. Even if we were believed on the basis of meagre evidence and, always belittled, intuition: the media is full of cases where the perpetrator is virtually "rewarded" by inadequate retribution. Indeed there was a recent case where neglect and assault in a nursing home led to a "punishment" of four months suspended sentence and a derisory fine of £150 for the two lives lost. Seventy five pounds – the value society puts on a life spent in its service.

We were still at an impasse when fate again intervened,

in the form of Gladys' attempted suicide. This was a matter for some doubt by the authorities, since an overdose was involved. Therefore it was easier and more comfortable to consider the incident a mishap. I don't know how anyone could consider swallowing a whole bottle of tablets an accident, but a vigilant milkman raised the alarm and an ambulance was called.

The pills might have done their job given more time. As it was the unpleasant but effective application of a stomach pump had saved her life. Many people went along with the confusion theory, including Gladys herself, but I knew better. Maggie Norris had succeeded where a lifetime of hardship and tragedy had failed: she had taken away her dignity and with it the will to live.

We immediately drove to the hospital to visit Gladys and offer what comfort and help we could. Aunt Dot provided the former whilst I made myself useful by volunteering to collect essential toiletries and personal items from home.

When I arrived at the house I recognised a familiar car parked a little way down the road. I had only seen the vehicle once before, but it was a distinctive bright red sports car which craved attention. On the earlier occasion it had been parked directly outside Gladys' home and my aunt had bitterly identified it as the carer's. Suspicions aroused I quietly walked around to the back door of the property, saw an empty kitchen through the window, gently placed the key in the lock and turned it.

The first thing I noticed on entering the kitchen was a conveniently spacious black bag on the table. What an opportunity. I paused and listened for any movement within the house. After a few seconds which passed like hours, I detected a faint noise coming from upstairs. It sounded like drawers being opened: surprise, surprise. I have always carried gloves but until recently seldom worn them. Now seemed such a moment. My immediate thought was to check for any stolen property as I moved towards temptation.

My first reaction was disappointment at the lack of evidence, but then I noticed something else. There was some sort of book slipped just inside: a diary or journal which might prove revealing. I paused again: the intruder had moved on to the wardrobe judging by the swishing of coat hangers. With more care than my partner in crime upstairs, I took out the book and soon realised that it was indeed a work schedule with a weekly record of clients.

Like the gloves I carry a mobile 'phone which is also rarely used. The 'phone itself is used for requirement, rather than as a replacement for face to face conversation. Regarding its other functions: I don't think I have sent a dozen texts in my life. There is something for me about the use of shortened phonetic messages which grates. The alternative lengthy text messages are therefore a waste of my time, when an email or 'phone call would be more efficient and less aggravation.

I do, however, know how to use the photographic facility. Cameras and their creations have been a delight since childhood. I have followed them through all their developments and manifestations. So, of course, one of my first tasks with any mobile is to personalise the screen. I realised I could now use this knowledge to duplicate the current page of her timetable. I dug in my handbag for the buried 'phone, and quickly scrolled through the icons. A few more clicks, and mission accomplished; I carefully returned my mobile and her journal to their respective bags.

In delving once more into her possessions I noticed an interesting item almost hidden in all the detritus at the bottom. A miniature version of the journal – recognisable as an address book. I just managed to extract this before I heard the telltale creaking of stair treads. Slipping the small object into my pocket, I moved backwards and opened the kitchen door. When she came into the kitchen she found me standing in the entrance. She obviously thought as I intended, that I had just arrived. Nevertheless she could not resist flashing a quick look to check her apparently undisturbed bag.

We both made swift explanations for our presence. I had the easier task, since I quite truthfully, said I was collecting items for the hospital. Norris, on the other hand, gave a waffle of lies consisting of some dubious fabrication about forgetting something on her last visit. I hardly listened: my mind was preoccupied with her book, which felt like it was trying to burn a hole out of my pocket. I suspect it would have been impossible to guess who was more relieved when she grabbed her bag and pushed past me.

I have to confess there was some satisfaction later when I recalled that I had stolen from a thief. There was a sort of poetic justice in this observation. I just hoped that the book would not be missed too quickly.

At the moment though I had work to do and, finding myself alone, collected the list of articles requested by Gladys. After gathering the usual toiletries, nightdress, etc., I grabbed the last item – her handbag. As I did an envelope fell out onto the floor: instead of the usual four/five line address it simple stated "To whom it may concern".

This was proving a day guaranteed to try even the least inquisitive nature!

I had a fair idea of the contents, but wanted confirmation. If I was going to plan some form of retribution I needed to be sure that it was justified. It was too easy: the note had been written in haste and the flap remained unsealed. The words, though written with difficulty, because of physical impairment and emotional strain, were a clear accusation.

A catalogue of brutality and betrayal. When I placed the letter back in its envelope I had my answer.

Back at the hospital I handed Gladys her bag without any comment, or sign I knew its significance. I was in no doubt whatsoever that the note would be retrieved and destroyed. It was much better this way. I was determined that both my aunt and Gladys would remain innocent of any involvement in my plans. As yet I had no idea what these would be, but, thanks to my pilfering I now had a starting point. I was more convinced than ever that this was not an isolated or random case of abuse. In my pocket I held a possible key to the solution – a potential list of fellow victims.

That evening, after supper, we both agreed that after the commotion of the day we needed an early night. This suited me just fine. But far from quickly "succumbing to the arms of Orpheus" I used the opportunity to explore my theory. In any case my mind was too lively for sleep. So I pulled out my mobile 'phone and copied out the entries from Norris' schedule. I now had two documents to compare, and placed my handwritten notes alongside the address book. It was easy enough to marry up the appointments with their corresponding names and addresses, so I added these details to my notes.

While doing this I noticed oddities in the address book. Some entries were marked with an asterisk. Obviously some personal code, the connotation of which I could not begin to interpret. As it turned out I was wrong to dismiss the significance of these marks so casually. My mind satisfied I slept like the proverbial log. Just as well, my next step meant a busy day tomorrow.

After dropping my aunt back at the hospital I spent the next day driving around on a reconnaissance: or "sussing out" mission: as I was in theory a criminal I may as well use their parlance. With my notes on the passenger seat and sat nav on the dashboard I followed Norris' weekly routine.

Looking for what? I'm not sure I knew myself yet, but felt that the answer lay in learning more about Norris and her activities. I soon found out one fact: her clients all lived within a tight geographical area. So it was that in a short space of time I found myself halfway through the schedule. I had left behind the rows of Edwardian terraced housing and more modern semi detached homes which made up the town centre. I was now being directed into the leafy suburbs, where tree lined quiet streets partially obscured large detached residences. Suddenly the sat nav announced I had reached my destination outside a three storey Victorian property. I began to change down the gears with the intention to park, but one glance at the house jerked my foot down on the accelerator. What I had experienced was a strong case of deja vu – for there on the gravel driveway was a familiar red sports car.

I drove further along the road, rounded a corner and parked. Once I had got my breath and senses back, I double checked the notes and confirmed that this was wrong. This visit was not part of the carer's normal rounds. There could be several explanations, but only one which fitted Norris hidden agenda.

What to do next? Well it would be the sensible course to just continue on my way. But when I looked at the notes to check the timetable I saw the "borrowed" address book sticking out of my bag. An idea began to form, and if this went to order it was a perfect solution. The plan was not without its risk, or even actual danger, but so beautiful in its simplicity that I would barely have to lift a finger. Like Derek Jones before her, Maggie Norris would bring about her own punishment. Her actions would also determine the severity of that sentence.

I left my car where it was and retraced my route back to the house. I had taken the precaution of donning my "hoodie" disguise, discarded my handbag and placed essential items in the pockets of my jacket. As I set off down the road I was bracing myself to encounter other pedestrians or traffic. With my camouflage I hardly looked a reputable character to be walking in such a prestigious neighbourhood, but then I didn't look like an innocent lady of a certain age either and that suited me perfectly. I need not have worried, there was absolutely no traffic, foot or mechanised, in sight. It was a quiet weekday and a quick glance as I walked into the driveway showed no movement – not even the twitch of lace curtains. No doubt this was the very reason Norris had felt safe in selecting this property for extra curriculum activity.

My only concern was "would she answer the door". If she didn't then nothing was lost except a wonderful opportunity.

There appeared to be no door bell, only an ornate lion knocker, which looked contemporary with the house. I confidently grasped this with my gloved hand and gave a meaningful thump. A few suspenseful moments later, I was considering repeating the exercise, when I heard footsteps on a tiled hallway. The door opened a few inches and I regarded my quarry. I had the advantage since I was expecting her, whereas she was taken off guard. Give her due though, she recovered amazingly well from the shock: probably a essential skill when engaged in felonious pursuits. Surprise rapidly gave way to confusion when she recognised my features through the gap.

I was practised and ready to respond. I explained, without great detail, that I had found her address book, but did not produce it for confirmation. I needed to get inside that house, and her first instinct might be to grab the article and slam the door in my face. I was ready with further excuses, but they were unnecessary. Norris' curiosity outweighed any uneasiness. She was certainly not frightened of me and now her crafty mind was functioning fully, would want the answer to certain questions. She widened the doorway and let me in. The trap was opening, but I was not yet sure who was the bait.

We went down the hall to the kitchen, where I finally handed back the address book. She returned it to the black bag, which today, I noted, was sitting on an antique Welsh dresser. Another part of my plan clicked satisfactorily into place.

An awkward silence ensued, so quiet I imagined I could hear the cogs in her brain turning. Then she broke the mood by asking the "million dollar question" : how had I known where she was? I could have embroidered the truth with some tale about getting information from the address book, but I decided time was too short for waffle.

I cut off any more questions by confronting her with the theft of property. She, at least, had the decency, more likely arrogance, not to bother denying the accusation. So I moved on to the next stage of my own agenda: a proposition. I suggested a mutually beneficial solution: I would keep quiet about her criminal activities if she agreed to share the profits.

Blackmail is an ugly word but it didn't hold a candle to the look on Norris' face. So evil was that brief uncensored look, I had a fleeting fear that she might abandon her usual subtle approach in favour of physical violence. I was, however, not worried that she might call my bluff. She could hardly throw stones within her own personal glass house.

It was a few seconds of tension, which you could cut with a knife, before the malicious expression changed to a smile. I swear I could see the wheels of her devious brain revolving as she agreed. There were none of the expected protestations or arguments which, in itself, unnerved me. Then I realised, with a bit of a shock and a lot of indignation, that when she looked at me, she saw yet another gullible oldie to be manipulated.

We had both remained standing during these negotiations – 'high noon' across a wooden scullery table. Without conscious thought neither of us was willing to place themselves in a psychological position of weakness. On a purely practical basis, I was not intending to crane my neck looking up at her. At this point, though, Norris gestured for me to take a seat and, to any casual observer, the atmosphere relaxed. Not me, I knew that this was probably the most critical moment.

She suddenly seemed to have made a decision: beyond that of conceding half her illegal income. She became excessively animated, and enthusiastically suggested we seal the bargain with a drink – would brandy be all right? Norris even made a coarse joke about the old lady not minding: she was currently absent in hospital undergoing treatment for an embarrassing personal problem. The 'carer' went into too much crude detail about this – no doubt believing I would share her sick humour. She was making this easy for me. The trap was closing, but on whom?

She left the room, presumably to get the liquor. This gave me the first moment I had to think about the grave implications of my hastily devised scheme. Now we were reaching the point of no return – which would change one of our lives forever. One thing I was absolutely committed to: I had no intention of swallowing anything she offered me. The decision came down to either heading for the exit, or proceeding with the plan. By the time Norris returned, carrying two crystal glasses, pre filled with some innocent looking amber liquid, I had made my choice.

As she came into the kitchen I was caught in the act of returning to my chair. She also registered my furtive glance towards her bag, which was still on the dresser. The address book was lying on the floor. Give her credit, without missing a beat, she brought the drinks over the table and placed mine in front of me. Suddenly I felt a surge of excitement which must have been an adrenaline boost. It was still not too late. If she ignored the lure, or kept her glass, I would have to beat a hasty retreat and regroup. As it was she did neither: she left her drink on the table and went over to recover her possession. I had not misjudged her, but she had seriously underestimated me. The difference being that I recognised her as a self centred, grasping individual, whereas she saw me as a stereotype.

With her back momentarily turned, and her mind preoccupied with retrieving the priceless book, this was the moment I imagined. Swopping drinks always seems so easy an exercise in books and films. In reality – well in fact it was. With one swift look at Norris I gently picked up both glasses and exchanged their positions. There was nothing, I could see, which distinguished one from the other. All the while I was nervously waffling on about how I saw the bag fall and tried to catch it.She didn't believe a word.

When she returned to the table I was already sipping away at my drink: I hoped, in a persuasive impersonation of a very tense person. Not too much acting required under the circumstances.

We sat opposite each other, talking and drinking, as if old friends. But I could see her watching me intently. Like a cat watching a mouse: timing its moment to spring. This nightmare seemed to go on for ages until I could no longer bear to make conversation, or even look at her. I was just beginning to think I should make my excuses and leave when she spoke.

Well it wasn't so much speech as one barely audible slur: "bitch". I stared at her to check that I heard correctly. What I saw in her face was at last a genuine reflection of her soul – for want of a better word. It was shockingly hideous: a mixture of fury and fear. Realisation had dawned that she was experiencing the symptoms she had anticipated for me. Norris tried to lunge forward, but was hampered by whatever substance she had mixed in my drink. The spirit was willing, but the body was failing. When I stared into her eyes, I saw nothing left but pure terror.I confess it was satisfying to see that emotion – it was one which she had inflicted on so many others.

The end came quickly, and with no evident physical pain. She was obviously a very proficient practitioner in her craft. Her mental anguish though must have been exquisite. I sat and watched her die with no special emotion. It was enough to know that Gladys, and her fellow sufferers, would now be safe. As the light went out of her eyes, I reflected that the last face she saw, and the last voice she heard, would be mine. One "old" person, whom she at last, but too late, recognised as someone worthy of respect : her executioner.

I left her on the floor where she had slipped and belonged. I left the house the same way I had come: the neighbourhood was still deserted. It wasn't until I was safely back in the car that I had a sobering thought. What if there had been a double bluff, and she had guessed I would switch glasses. Well it would now be my body lying on the kitchen floor. Although, knowing Norris' resourcefulness and strength, I imagine my corpse would soon have found an ignominious resting place.

What ifs, however, are too time consuming as you grow older. As it was she fell into her own trap. She dismissed me as another faceless pensioner, albeit an avaricious one. Nevertheless an over 60 something and therefore brain cell challenged. Not so stupid though: I took the incriminating glass, which I later rinsed and slipped into a city centre recycling bin. I had left no trace, even if experts looked for it: all those episodes of C.S.I., had been worthwhile beyond entertainment.

Only her body remained for discovery at some later date. When her presence in an unoccupied property would be a cause for suspicion as much as surprise. For the moment though I made a cautious journey home. The last thing I needed was to be stopped and breathalysed. With the amount of brandy consumed, I could not guarantee the results.

As with my previous venture into sudden death, my only concern was for the unfortunate person who next opened that front door. If most accidents at home, then, in my experience, the kitchen must be the most popular room. It may be a long wait, and with the warmer weather arriving it would not be a welcoming homecoming.

As luck would have it though, rigor mortis barely had time to set in. The very next day a welfare worker called to collect the post and got considerably more than she bargained for. Luckily she was a middle aged ex-military type with a strong constitution, so no lasting harm was done. In fact, judging by the neighbourhood grapevine, it proved quite a source of stimulation for the next month.

There were still a few days to run on my extended visit, so I was relieved that I would no longer have to wait for news second hand. Although there was nothing to tie me to Norris except a chance meeting at Gladys', I had a natural interest in the enquiry. If I do say so myself, I made a professional job of feigning shock and surprise at the unfolding events. I was either becoming an accomplished actress – or liar.

Ah, but again kismet. As I guessed, Maggie Norris was a serial criminal, whose offences ranged much farther in area and severity than anyone imagined. It transpired that several police forces were already looking into her activities. Luckily for me, lack of evidence and manpower had made physically following her movements impracticable.

The recovery of the address book was a vital piece in the puzzle. My indecipherable asterisks did indeed have a sinister significance. They marked all those 'clients' whose wills included bequests to Maggie Norris.

No one would probably ever be sure of the real extent of her iniquity. Murder: well many people doubted they had such a monster in their midst. I made no comment, but could have been a first hand witness to her capabilities in that direction. One fact remained: she had left a trail of deceased patients around the country. Whether she hastened that process, or was merely fortunate in her charges fatalities, remains a nationwide official investigation.

She chose her victims carefully: they were all terminally ill and already on morphine. Her weapon of choice, and probably the cause of her own demise. She did her homework well, and ensured there were no known relatives or close friends who might dispute her claim. When she began this career no-one will probably uncover, because she was content with petty pilfering. Even her initial foray into the inheritance industry was conducted with restraint: limited to small legacies. But with success grew conceit and greed had got the better of her. Flags started to be raised when bequests grew from valuable jewellery to property. I had indeed judged my target well.

These disclosures provided a motive, not for murder but suicide. I could not believe my luck. Once more I had been spared the ordeal of uncomfortable questions. Perhaps, after all despite my doubts, there was some higher force at work.

If so they certainly had a sense of natural justice and black humour.

I stayed in the North long enough to welcome Gladys home. When the police searched Norris' flat they found several interesting items, including some familiar Wedgewood figurines. These were still in police custody but one item had been released. This, if you like, was my second trophy, although I would prefer the term 'treasure'.

The joy on Gladys' face when the stolen wedding ring was replaced on her finger.

Chapter Five

THE TRAVELLER'S TALE

I closed another satisfactory chapter in my new career and headed across the North/South divide. Yorkshire, courtesy of my paternal ancestors, will always be a special place for me. Unlike many critics, I love the native "call a spade a bloody shovel" attitude to life. Even their, frequently misunderstood, dour sense of humour is like a breath of fresh air. In my humble opinion, there is far too much so called "sophisticated" farce which relies on cruelty and malice. Of course, tragedy and comedy have traditionally been compliant partners, but the "little tramp" underdog was always the hero, never the brunt of ridicule.

After the long drive, I was glad to be back in the house I had always known as home. I was actually born in the front bedroom, when such events were the norm rather than the exception. One of my weaknesses, but a great virtue in my new illicit vocation, was tidiness. So my first job, even before the essential cuppa (back in the south now) was to empty the luggage and put away its contents.

Although I have seen quite a large segment of the world during my lifetime, I have always tried to avoid travel abroad in the Spring. It is, without consideration, my favourite season, although, sadly it seems to be in decline. Blame this on global warming, climate change, or whatever is currently the vogue: the result is the same. The months of March and April are being overtaken by winter, whilst premature summer claims May and June. Spring is increasingly squeezed between its more aggressive cousins. The fragility and rarity of its nature makes it all the more precious – at least for me. Others may worship the warmer, if not necessarily sunny, weather, but I have always loved the Spring.

I see it as the true beginning of the year. I am not a poet, but to wax lyrical: life is returning as animals and plants emerge from their shelters. Our senses are overwhelmed with its sights, sounds and scents. It is literally a breath of fresh air after seemingly endless dark and depressing days. Even for unbelievers Spring appears like a miracle: a promise fulfilled, a sign that God has not completely given up on us. Or to quote the late philosopher, Bernard Williams: " The day the Lord created hope was probably the same day he created Spring".

It is Nature's rush hour. All living things frantically meeting and mating to continue the circle of life. Even humanity, which has almost severed its ecological roots, becomes affected by the mood. While human beings have never needed any seasonal impetus to reproduce, nevertheless, they join the bustle. You only have to witness the sudden activity at DIY and Garden Centres to prove this fact.

After my recent activities in the North I needed some physical distraction and found it in my generous garden.

Fortunately, thanks to my green fingered grandmother, it is a mature garden (rather like its owner) which requires maintenance rather than expense. However hidden between all the budding bulbs, forget me nots and primroses, lurk the dreaded and flourishing weeds. I recall someone once said that a weed is just a wild flower in the wrong place. Regretfully some of these "wild flowers," usually the less aesthetically attractive, are by sod's law, the most proficient breeders. Ah, if only I was less environmentally fastidious with my weed killer as other poisons. Then life for my flowers – and back – would be as easy as it now was for Gladys.

And this Spring cleaning does not end at the back door. The fever gets into us beyond the normal change of curtains and bed linen. Suddenly the new bright sunlight assaults every neglected nook and cranny, detecting previously concealed blemishes. This year I was determined not to succumb to the Forth Bridge syndrome, where one piece of redecoration leads to complete renovation of the entire house. Instead I satisfied my urge with a splash of fresh paint and clean wallpaper in the hallway before the weather turned too humid. It could be a case of age or, more likely, extending waistline, but as I grow older, or fatter, the slightest exercise brings on an uncomfortable flush. I suppose I should describe this as glowing, in the words of the old adage "Horses sweat. Men perspire. But ladies merely glow". While I am definitely neither man nor horse, the term "lady" is a title I have never aspired to, so I think the word sweat would be a more accurate, if not so genteel, description.

Guilt pacified, with the commencement of June my thoughts turned to my holiday home on the West Wales coast. I had bought this static caravan several years ago, when the publishing business, which was my occupation, boomed. Although the park opened in March, between the inclement weather and the visit to my aunt, I had not yet made the five hour drive. Truth be told, it had become somewhat of a burden, with the yearly fees and mileage – making weekends, even long ones, an impractical expense. But it was still a relatively cheap vacation option: certainly more so than some friends who had become entangled in the "time share" web. Although I never anticipated the journey with any pleasure I knew that enjoyment would come once I got behind the wheel. Besides I looked forward to, what I hoped would be, a much needed break.

All went well on the first multi motorway stretch: with no dreaded illuminated signs warning "caution – queues – road works". As I left the northern route and turned west I began to see the first "think bike" signs. I have pondered why there are so few signs directed at the motor cyclists personally. It seems to imply that they have no brains to think for themselves – or absolutely no sense of self preservation. If I were, what is ironically called "a two wheel coffin" rider I would find either explanation insulting.

Perhaps the authorities just think it a means of dealing with diminishing eyesight, because sadly a good deal of the bad press for bikers comes from my own generation. There seems to be an increasing mid life crisis trend towards recapturing the "rocker" culture of fifties and sixties youth. Don't get me wrong I earnestly applaud the elderly of any generation in their quest not to be grounded. I sometimes even wish I had the nerve to face my fears and take up sky diving! My firm belief is in a fundamental right to pursue your life, or end it, as an individual choice. The problems arise when this conflicts with the safety of others.

I was still following this train of thought when a flock of said bikers swooped past me: anonymous in their predominantly black and red leather uniforms. I swerved a little as a "tail end Charlie" brought up the rear of the pack and wobbled precariously as he/she pulled back in front of me.

They accelerated away up the road and my mind turned to finding a half way house refreshment and toilet break. Knowing the route so well I remembered that there was just such a place nearby. Another half a mile brought me to the turn for Dinkys: a well known and loved spot for all travellers. In the secluded lay by you can find every range of transportation. Hauliers escaping from the cabs of their artics; holidaymakers with either overexcited or over tired children; business people saving on expenses. The modern equivalent of a coaching inn with all the time-honoured bustle. This vehicular melting pot would, of course, been incomplete without the obligatory parked up motor cycles and today was no exception.

As I stretched and extricated my body from its driving position, my eyes adjusted to sights other than an endless ribbon of tarmac. One I recognised immediately: a registration plate on one of the bikes which rang a mental bell and connected to the recent near miss. I felt no sense of outrage, but the unknown is always enticing and I was intrigued to see what lurked beneath the leather veneer. The pack had apparently ordered their brunch and were beginning to discard their helmets in readiness to eat. As they removed the protective fibreglass cocoons, what emerged was not so much Marlon Brando or Marianne Faithfull, as Victor Meldrew and Hyacinth Bouquet. Despite my earlier musings I was still mesmerized by the incongruity of the scene. It was rather like following a sylph like figure with flowing blonde locks along the pavement, only to discover they belonged to an eighty year old woman, or man!

Oh well, good for them I thought, and returned to minding my own business, by ordering a burger and mug of tea. I found a place on an adjacent table, in all honesty, not with any intention of eavesdropping. As it turned out with the volume level of the conversation I could have sat back in my car and overheard. My ears pricked up because the gist seemed to centre around the incident which involved me. A post mortem (perhaps inappropriate term in the circumstances) concluded that these "modern" bikes were perhaps a tad too powerful. Mutual reminiscences followed about narrow escapes on bends. I suddenly saw the long and winding road ahead of me, and made a quick decision. The bikers were well settled into their meal and recollections, so I burnt my oesophagus swigging down the hot drink and headed back to the car. The burger could be devoured en route. I would rather risk that distraction than a further clash with my lunch companions.

The next part of my journey although only 75 miles, I knew would take as long as the previous 120. Proof, I suppose, that motorways have the advantage, although I do not like driving on them. It is too easy to get lulled into a semi hypnotic state, which can lead to dangerous or stupid decisions. Several times in the past I have found myself taking the wrong exit, either through misreading the signs, or, more likely, being blocked by large vehicles. An inexperienced or bad driver on a normal road becomes a serious hazard on a motorway and when there are hold ups they can be spectacular.

However, there is the bonus that slower traffic can be negotiated, not such an easy manoeuvre on the main route to West Wales. A series of single lane A roads, which begin in the beautiful green undulations of the borderlands and become dramatically breathtaking in the Snowdonia National park around Dolgellau.

Unfortunately the fact that it is the primary road for all traffic, as well as a main tourist route, leads to many problems. On bad days I have found myself stuck behind a sluggish convoy headed by the dreaded camper van, farm tractor, or even artic. On really bad days all three! Market days will add trailers of doomed livestock to the procession. However the alternative would be an unthinkable devastation of the surrounding countryside. In any case the journey is usually an all or nothing affair and on this occasion my drive to "civilization" was relatively stress free.

I arrived within the usual five hour schedule and spent a peaceful and restful week. Some days I chose to explore the woodlands and mountains: other times turned westwards towards the beaches and sea. The weather co-operated: warm, but tolerable temperatures, with some showers, but mainly sunshine. No conditions too extreme to keep me indoors for shelter or comfort.

By the time I contemplated the return journey I was thoroughly chilled and, I thought, prepared to face the worst of human nature. I spent a leisurely last day: cleaning the caravan, washing and replacing the linen. All the day to day grind I had avoided during the week. I finished up the fridge debris for tea, packed the rest in the car and was on the road by 7pm. I hoped that my decision to delay the drive back would avoid the worst traffic – and even worst behaviour. Well, as the saying warns, "we live in hope, and die in despair".

The reversed cross country route was uneventful and, after a brief pause at Dinkys, I reached the first motorway as the sun was slowly sinking. Another hour and another motorway found me negotiating the increasingly thinning traffic by the beam of my headlights. If I say so myself: I would never fail a driving test for forgetting to look in the rear view mirror. To the point that I am always critical of t.v. dramas in which drivers neglect to notice a shadowing car. So when I was temporarily blinded by the reflection of full beam headlights in said mirror it was a shock. In the words of so many accident insurance claims "it seemed to appear from nowhere".

I estimated that it must be a large vehicle, judging by the height of the beams, but not a lorry. I barely had time to register this before the vehicle swerved out into the central lane and I could see it was a dark foreign built SUV.

As it accelerated past me the driver fumbled the gears and this hesitationgave me a chance to sneak a sideways glance. Despite night overtaking us we were on a well lit part of the motorway and in those few seconds I saw more than enough to rocket my adrenalin level. As the driver passed me I saw the outline of a bottle, which shared his grip with the steering wheel. Meanwhile his "free" hand held a mobile 'phone tightly against the side of his obviously brainless head.

I was still digesting this image as the rear of the SUV

drew level with me and delivered a further jolt. In the back seat, just visible above the door frame, stared a pair of small terrified eyes. I could not believe what I was seeing. Yet, as if in mockery, a sign in the back window confirmed my fears with the proud boast "child on board".

I watched the car weaving dangerously between the other, thankfully, few vehicles on the carriageway. I caught my breath as I saw bright red brake lights come on, and then released the air as the 4x4 successfully made the manoeuvre onto an exit ramp.

I didn't even spare time for a thought, my reaction was pure instinct. I pressed my left indicator and followed the vehicle towards the welcoming lights of a Services area.

I quickly slowed down to comply with the speed restrictions: which gave me the opportunity to scan the parking spaces. It was relatively quiet and most of the illumination came from the buildings and lamps dotting the area. There were certainly no headlights or interior lights evident in the unpromising darkness, just the dark silhouettes of deserted vehicles.

I knew these services well: I had paused here many times to fill my tank. So I negotiated my car through the fringes of the park, where I knew there were no telltale surveillance cameras. I came to a halt near a spot, which I knew doubled as the dog walking and picnic area. During the daylight hours this attractive landscaped area was a busy spot, now it looked deserted and sinister. In any other circumstances it would have been my last choice, but now it was perfect.

I parked up in a corner space, and rolled down the window before turning off the engine. I took a deep refreshing breath of the cool night air to clear my lungs and mind. What to do now? There was no sign of a dark, or even light, SUV among the cars in front of me. I was just getting my brain in gear and thinking of following suit with the car when I heard a voice. It was not too close, but, liberated by anger and alcohol, it was loud enough to hear the gist. "Shut up you little bastard or I'll really give you something to fucking cry about".

There were two items I needed from the boot, and considered my options. I could disable the interior light but not so easily mute the sound of doors slamming. Luckily this was a hatchback so I had another route which attracted less attention. I am neither so flexible nor fit as in my youth when shifting about a car was an easy matter, but I was still game.

The tricky part was extricating my legs without defeating the object by accidentally hitting the horn. With a great deal of care, and minimum bruising from contact with the gear stick and handbrake, I crawled between the front seats. Now I regretted that last burger: "A moment on the lips, a lifetime on the hips" was proved accurate as I was forced to slide sideways onto the rear seats. It was a relatively simple matter to lift the back cover and remove the equipment. Even hampered by these objects the reversed scramble was much easier.

Now I switched off the interior light. I looked around, then gently opened the driver's door and closed, rather than slammed, it behind me. Despite the excuses of noisy motorists, it is actually possible to do this. The open window I had to leave, if events went as planned, this would be the least of my problems!

In my trusty hoodie I walked behind the car. There was

no point in prowling around, such behaviour would in itself draw attention. I may as well put a neon sign above my head "up to no good".

At this point I can honestly state that my intention was to confirm my concerns before transferring the execution of justice to the authorities.

I took one final look around and disappeared into the bushes. The voice was now quieter, more conversational in tone. I followed the sound, occasionally scanning with the binoculars I had removed from my boot. The third sweep I saw it. The vehicle was parked in the "caravans only" designated area. There was no visual of the driver, but a monologue was emulating from a small copse of trees directly in front of me. Now I adopted "stealth" mode and crept forwards. As I entered the thicket I saw him: standing a few yards away with his back to me. Both the bottle, now distinguishable as Vodka, and mobile 'phone continued to be clenched in each hand. The latter still appeared to be glued to his ear and he was talking into it. Although his speech volume was low somehow this fact enhanced, rather than softened, the sense of menace.

If the man's previous drunken, violent behaviour had already sickened me, then the situation was about to sink to a completely new depth of revulsion.

The one sided part of the dialogue I overheard told me all I needed to know about the monster.

He was obviously addressing the child's mother – or rather threatening her. There was no doubt that he was the woman's pimp, as well as enjoying additional benefits. Since it became clear that he was the father of the innocent in the car. No doubt the birth of the child had provided the courage formerly suppressed and she had left him. She fastened her baby, and loaded a few personal possessions from a previous life, into the SUV. Judging by his words it was this loss, rather than his daughter, which had fuelled his quest for retribution.

It had taken him a while to find them. All her "work" colleagues, might be dismissed as whores by their clients and pimps, but they possessed a morality unknown by the parasites who fed off them. To their everlasting credit, to a woman, they steadfastly refused to submit to whatever persuasion was employed. No, it was ironically the means of her liberation which had also been her downfall. The one traceable link had been the vehicle registration. With the help of a few equally minded friends he boasted how he found her.

But there would be no swift reckoning. Revenge is a dish best served cold, and the chase had given him time to contemplate. His conclusion chilled me to the bone. God only knows what it did to the mother at the other end of that technological instrument of torture. Her punishment would be through the child she had escaped to protect.

No, he said with sickening relish, she would never see her little girl again. He knew some men, although no decent person would describe them so, who perversions fed on the most weak and vulnerable. His child would fetch a good price. Even with my enlightened view on the depravities of human nature I could not believe my ears. He went on to describe in cruel and obscene graphic detail the future of her daughter. This proved the catalyst for what followed

He was so absorbed in verbally twisting the knife in his one time "lover" that he never heard me come up behind him. Up close he was a remarkably large and powerful man, but so was Goliath. I had no slingshot, but I did have a wheel brace: the second item I had taken from my boot. I had carried the tool for my protection, but now defended another. Fury and adrenaline fuelled my strength as I raised the weapon and brought it down on his skull. One blow would not have sufficed, but pure rage rather than reason, provided the solution. By the time my temper was exhausted there was no doubt as to the extinction of life.

Drained I stood over the body from which I had taken life. What did I feel: not guilt or even regret. Shock perhaps – astonishment certainly. This was after all a real murder: up close and personal. The first time I had literally got my hands dirty. That expression brought common sense to the fore, and I realised this was in fact probably true. Suddenly I felt physically contaminated. I touched my face but could feel no accusatory splatter. A look down at my protected body and hands revealed nothing in the darkness. In the middle of these observations came a sound which jolted me out of this night dream. I was already concocting an explanation when I realised it was the dropped mobile.

I am not an expert chess player, but my limited experience in the game has taught me the process of thinking at least a few moves ahead. I used this training now in my present dilemma. I was a good enough mimic: I could disguise my voice to give our location without risk to myself. This move would ensure the child's safety, but think it through. The hysterical mother would undoubtedly rush to the scene and I would then be placing her in danger. Even given the mitigating circumstances, or even because of them, she may be seen as the chief suspect. I weighed the safety of the child against that of her mother and discounted that strategy. The pair's happiness was inextricably bound together. Decision made I picked up the 'phone and silently turned it off.

I paused a moment before dropping the 'phone back to its owner. It contained nothing incriminating: in fact it would help reunite mother and child. The recipient of the last call could be traced, which in turn would eliminate the woman by providing a watertight alibi. Perfect, I had made my opening move.

Now I tried to look around the "crime scene" objectively, as I imagined the police investigators eventually would. I began at the main focus – the body. No evidence there, except for the indentations of the wheel brace. Would this provide some clue to my car? I thought not. Wheel braces are specific to nuts and bolts not the make of vehicle. I knew this because when I obtained my car second hand it was one of the missing accessories. A nuisance at the time, I never thought this omission would prove so useful.

Repressing the urge to flee I forced myself to study the area – like a student memorising an exam paper for later reflection. I could see nothing which would provide a trace to my identity. I returned my attention to the corpse and in my peripheral vision caught sight of my feet. Footprints. It was dry weather and the ground looked firm, but there would be marks. What would they show? The treads of size 6 (to allow for extra socks) trainers, which could be found in hundreds of high street and mall shops around the country. I am not sure they would even provide accurate gender confirmation. But paranoia was taking hold. Did the soles contain some miniscule grain of sand or soil which would follow me home? Indeed the footprints themselves would lead back to my parking space – what information would that supply? Nothing! Then I thought once more of the body. The attack and blood distribution would of course indicate the height and strength of the assailant. With an effort I metaphorically took hold of the panic and clawed back my self control. These things I could not change, and interference would only spotlight these facts.

No when you lose a needle it is better to do so in an haystack. The man was evil, but I could not rely on the authorities recognising the poetic justice of his demise. Neither could I disguise his death as anything other than murder. Suicide was a physical impossibility even for a contortionist. Accident – well it would require an imagination much greater than the police or mine to come up with a plausible scenario. Even a plea of self defence would be pointless given the nature of the injuries.Murder was the only feasible conclusion.

But I could create my own camouflage by muddying the already murky waters. Here was a man who lived on the edge. A man who would have numerous enemies of both sexes. If I left him now the perpetrators would be plentiful, but if I added robbery to the mix the suspect pool would become an ocean. And if my name did surface what was my motive except the coincidence of being in the right place at the wrong time.

I would leave the mobile. In doing so the police might well suspect that the robbery was staged, but they could not dismiss the suggestion out of hand.. Bracing myself I searched through his pockets, careful to avoid contamination. I removed the wad of cash I found in his wallet, and the seemingly expensive wristwatch.

I had one more task. I could not leave the child in the car at the mercy of a fickle fate, or insensitive God. While I might have little morality left, determination to protect the innocent was a fundamental justification of my new path. It was what still distinguished me from most serial killers, along with a complete lack of ego. In fact just the opposite: I would rather hide my work than require public recognition. Nevertheless I could no longer deny that I had now joined that, fortunately, exclusive company.

What could I do to bring attention to the child while protecting myself? Then it came to me. Had the brute appreciated his daughter's monetary and reprisal value enough to keep her secured within the vehicle? In other words – would he have armed the doors.?

I crept back through the undergrowth towards the large dark SUV, picking up a large rock as I went. The shrubbery stopped just feet from the back of the vehicle. All was silence. I was sorry for any further distress I would cause the solitary occupant, but needs must when the devil drives. Well this devil was currently a few yards away and, like most dead carcasses, had found his true vocation. There is only one great leveller, despite claims of a more equal society – death. Whether we end up in Westminster Abbey, or a pauper's grave our physical fate is the same. One way or another we return to earth from which we came. For whether we like it or not we are just part of the cycle of the universe, not its axis. *"Ashes to ashes, dust to dust, if god won't have ye, the devil must!"* Anon.

I lifted the rock and very cautiously aimed the missile at the driver's door.

It had the desired effect, but the commotion still startled

me back into the bushes. Leaving the headlights flashing like white neons, and the alarms producing a racket which could have accompanied a prison break, I retraced my route.

It took several tense minutes to reach my own, thankfully, undisturbed car. I removed my gloves and stowed them in my pockets, before following suit with the jacket. This article I turned inside out, wrapping the wheel brace within it, and placed all incriminating evidence on the back seat.

Finally I turned the starter once, allowing me to rewind the window, without igniting the engine: before slumping back into the driver's seat. Although cloaked in the darkness, I took the precaution of adopting the pretence of sleep. I was far enough away, and screened, from the loudly protesting vehicle, for this to be convincing. All the time I watched the distant buildings for any sign of activity.

It was thankfully a quiet night at the services, so it wasn't long before two figures emerged from the illuminated entrance. The binoculars established that they were a brace of security guards: one male, one female. A partnership designed to deal with any emergency and perfect for the dilemma I had created.

They disappeared out of my line of vision towards the focus of their fortunately undivided attention. It seemed an age before they silenced the alarm and another aeon before I saw the pair once more. Except this time they had become a "family". One of the security guards now clutched a small bundle to their chest. A surreptitious look with the binoculars confirmed the impression that it was the woman carrying the toddler. The poor little girl was obviously frightened and confused, but she clung to her saviour with a fierce determination.

I had seen what I hoped, as I watched the trio enter the shelter of the buildings. But I waited a few more moments. During that interval my priorities turned again to self preservation. If would be ironic if, after seemingly getting away with murder, I was pulled over on a police check and found to be literally red faced. I needed to check for any incriminating blemishes, but I could not risk the interior light. Instead I groped around in the glove compartment and extracted my trusty mini Mag. A further forage in my handbag produced a rarely used cosmetic mirror. Utilisation of these two items was not easily accomplished in the cramped well of the front passenger seat, but it did eventually provide reassurance. I replaced both the torch and mirror, gave a mental sigh, and drove away.

The remainder of the journey was uneventful, but required enough concentration to distract my mind from conducting an autopsy. It was almost another day by the time I reached home. But one of my many flaws is a compulsion to tidy up. "Tomorrow is another day" has no part in my philosophy. So I unpacked the car, including the accusatory items on the back seat, which I stuffed into a black bag. A decision about these could wait until the morning – when my thoughts were fresh. It had been a long day in more ways than one! A final chore remained before climbing the wooden hill to Bedfordshire. Mine is an old Edwardian home, well built and spacious, but built at a time when plumbing was restricted to the kitchen and outside privy. So I drew an environmentally unfriendly large bath of water in the downstairs extension and washed away any bodily evidence.

That night I surprised myself by sleeping the sleep of the

just. No nightmares, or even, dreams disturbed my slumber. Where was my conscience – merely having a siesta, or completely comatose.

Either way it certainly did not wake up with the rest of me. A post mortem brought no feelings of guilt, only concern that there may, after all, have been evidence of my presence. Tidying up loose ends, first thing the next day I thoroughly washed my coat and its contents. The wheel brace I scoured and returned to my boot. I had considered disposal, but then I would have to purchase a replacement, which may in turn provide a trail. My beloved coat and gloves were consigned to a Salvation Army charity bin. I decided that it was safe enough to replace these without incurring any suspicion. So I was now fairly sure that there was little physical connection to the crime, but what about my vehicle?

One belated thought came to me "were there CCTV cameras leading to and from the motorway?" If so my registration would be as unique and damning as fingerprints. This led to the anxiety that if police then scanned other cinematic footage of the car park they would find no corresponding plate. Of course they would then turn their attention to more remote locations. This extended search, together with my footprints, would direct detectives to my former parking spot like beacons.

By this time these nagging thoughts, combined with an overactive imagination, had already led an arresting officer to my door. OK, so accepting the worst – what would happen next? Of course I would go to prison, even without the authorities' knowledge of my other "offences". I had killed what society considered a "fellow human being." But how long would that sentence be? Could I plead any mitigating circumstances? Certainly not self defence – some rather obvious craters in the back of his cranium would discount that plea. No I would have to "come clean," and hope the extenuating circumstances of genuine irrepressible frenzy would soften the charge from murder to manslaughter. The mother could definitely bear witness to the horror of the conversation I had overheard.

Any jury may feel pity, but they would not stretch to innocence. I would serve a sentence, and at my age it may as well be death. But, as many guilty people will admit, they are not sorry for the crime, only getting caught. When I went back over my own offence I understood exactly what they meant. As far as I was concerned it was neither murder, nor manslaughter, but execution. I could not even begin to consider what would have happened if I had let that creature drive away. A thing who deserved justice because somewhere in his ancestors' evolution they had mastered the skill of walking on two legs. No, even if I did not judge my actions a crime, I was willing to do the time – even if it used every minute I had left.

In a very short time I gone through all stages more normally associated with grief and arrived at acceptance. There was nothing more to do but wait. At least from my previous experiences I was getting quite familiar, even comfortable, with this process. I had already learnt to push pointless worries into a cupboard at the back of my mind, which I usually kept shut. So my life continued as normal, except for one extra daily chore.

Every morning I googled through all the national online newspapers, and included media web sites specific to the services location. If I could not escape the legal repercussions of my actions, then I, at least, wanted to anticipate the knock on my door.

I stopped my newspaper delivery several years ago. Everyone has to earn a living, and I have nothing but respect for the dedication and bravery of ethical journalists. But as with every commendable profession there are those who manipulate this power for less noble ends. Whether due to my own cynicism, or reality, I see a growing trend towards sensationalism at the expense of truth. The result of this manipulation all too often this seems to create further suffering rather promote a remedy.

It never ceases to amaze me that important genuine news stories seem to be overlooked and never see the light of day. Instead many papers are crammed with Z list celebrity gossip and photographs which should really be confined to the newsagents' top shelf. However, in this instance, I had reason to be grateful for this neglect. Days went by without one editorial word, let alone the accusatory headline I had dreaded.

A week later I was preparing to permanently seal that cupboard door, when a search on a local news site drew my attention. A small article slipped into the latter digital pages, which I would have missed except for the accompanying image. Strangely enough the by line did not include the word "murder." Instead the story centred on the reunion of a kidnapped child with its mother. Brief mention was made of the father, who was accurately described as a lowlife and perpetrator of the crime. With less truth the tale continued to its satisfying conclusion: where the offender met his fitting nemesis during an aggravated robbery.

Now I could see the woman whose voice I heard faintly over the ether in another age. A time before I crossed the line which made me a murderer. A young face, but probably actually younger than she looked. A woman who could not hide the disillusionment in eyes which had seen too much despair in her short life.

But there was something else there which was shared with the tiny replica she held tightly in her arms. Both the mother and child looked at the camera, which does sometimes lie, but in this case truly recorded what it captured. Love.

I took one final look at the photograph before closing the page. I thought briefly about printing a copy, but not for long. There was no point, it had already been embedded in my mental scrapbook.

Chapter Six

THE MINSTREL'S TALE

With some lingering doubts that the news report did not in fact disclose the full police investigation, I settled down to try and enjoy the remaining summer months.

Although in reality the onset of any period of fine weather is not a guarantee of bliss, and certainly not a time to enjoy peace and quiet. This year summer consisted of a few warm, dry days scattered through July and August. It is a fact that most eagerly anticipated events deprive more pleasure from the journey than arrival. This case was no different. Almost as soon as the clouds cleared and nature emerged from the pall, so did pests like wasps and mosquitoes. At weekends these irritants were joined by their two legged comrades. Very soon after the first sun loungers had staked a claim on patios I began to yearn for the harmony that comes with isolation. Call me a grumpy old misery if you like, but I would reverse the words of Dante Alighieri, 13th century philosopher poet, who claimed that "The path to Paradise begins in Hell." The inferno in this instance was appropriately represented by innumerable fires smelling of charcoal and burnt flesh.

Australia has given us many wonderful and worthy exports, but, to my mind, barbies is not one of them. Perhaps they have lost something in the translation. My first introduction to the art of the barbeque was during gatherings hosted by an American offshoot to our family tree. Try as I may I cannot remember any desperation associated with igniting the charcoal, and no scents reminiscent of meths or even petroleum. I do recall, with mouth watering clarity, the resultant meal: succulent and crisp without cremation.

Unfortunately barbeques have now evolved into some sort of masculine rite of passage. Hunter gatherers have given way to an image of the male members of a family grouped around a smouldering BBQ. Unless they have conceded defeat and invested in a gas powered adaptation.Such conclaves are usually accompanied by producing enough cumulative air contamination to rival Chernobyl. Even with the amount of arsonist aids now widely available, what begins as lunch ends as supper. A meal which has the odd and unsettling combination of a black shell encircling a suspicious looking pink interior. In such cases you feel that the party invitation should come complete with an appointment at your local hospital A&E.

However by the time this charred excuse is ceremoniously presented to the diners, everyone is too marinated in booze to notice or care. There is a strange frenzied desperation to "enjoy oneself", or at least appear to be doing so. If good food and company fail to produce this, then copious amounts of alcohol produce the desired joie de vivre.

Of course this is true of most social events where

"adults" are involved regardless of season. Fortunately though, in this country, inclement weather usually keeps the released inhibitions safely indoors. In fine weather what begins outdoor continues outdoors, sometimes until the early hours.

Don't get me wrong: I enjoy a drink as much as the next one, as long as the next one isn't a candidate for the AA.

At this point our sense of smell has already been subjected to the fall out of air pollution. Now it is the turn of our ears to be bombarded by a combined onslaught of "music" and competing "human" accompaniment. I use the term music loosely, since the decibels are typically so high that all harmony is lost. What remains is the monotonous tortuous beat of the bass. I use the term "human" loosely, because the sound emulating from voice boxes capable of speech more accurately resembles a pack of rabid hyenas.

All this display of "high spirits" is bad enough when inflicted on the immediate neighbourhood. The problem is magnified tenfold when the mayhem spills out onto the street.

Younger delinquents are found at all hours on street corners and parks, making the most of their freedom. Older delinquents are more of a menace on four wheels, where the passengers, and even driver, are well on the road to inebriation. Commonsense then goes out the windows: drawing attention by revving engines, raucous horns and the inevitable stereo.

Daylight is no better. When the sun comes up, it does so to desolation on all fronts. Streets littered with more than, well litter! Substances, the second time around, if possible, even worse than the original BBQ. Now I suspect I know the true meaning of fast food, which has more to do with time it stays in the digestive system than its production.

As for the beauties of Nature. Any countryside walk is bound to the greeted with the debris from previous explorers. Metal, glass and plastic in all its infinite variety. Perhaps even the ruins of an impromptu rave complete with smoking fire and vandalised trees. No longer can you take a tranquil, restful stroll through the local woods. Instead you risk life and limb dodging arrogant "environmentally friendly" cyclists who do not see carving gouges through the undergrowth as in any way hypocritical.

At these times how I long for rain to douse the fires and drive people back into their caves.

So far our neighbourhood had been relatively free of such nuisances, but all this was about to change. We had started out with a huge advantage. Our suburb had developed from a Cotswold village, and the original dwellings still provided its core. These had been built at a time when land was less precious than the need for sufficient space to raise vegetables and chickens. With the advent of allotments and supermarkets, shrubbery and trees had long since replaced the more open plan landscape. Consequently the adjoining gardens were now long, and secluded, enough to provide enough privacy to easily screen a nudist colony.

In addition our status as a "conservation area" ensured that house prices remained too high for development opportunities. Even so, as some of the transient professionals moved onwards and upwards, they chose to lease rather than sell. So it was that we acquired our own small group of rental properties, which were mainly indistinguishable from those privately owned. Except for one – proving that there is always the exception to any rule. The owners, or their agents, were neglectful in terms of upkeep, hardly surprising then that they were similarly cavalier in their choice of tenant. We had managed to avoid the phenomena thus far, but now we found ourselves with our very own "neighbour from Hell". He moved in quietly enough shortly after my return from Wales. Or perhaps my mind was on other matters at that time. Initially all went well. Contact was made, and although my neighbours are not gregarious, they are hospitable individuals. Personally I had only seen the newcomer on a couple of occasions: the usual mumbled greetings as we passed in the street. This honeymoon period was very brief and lasted only as long as the first warm weekend.

The modus operandi was always the same. The first sign was music. This began softly at around lunch time: I suspect when he crawled out of his pit. From then on it escalated in tandem with the arrival of more friends. By teatime the noise was only avoidable by withdrawing indoors and closing all doors and windows. As darkness fell there was no escape. Even when the party disbanded in the early hours the tenant would collapse in the garden leaving the speakers blaring. Foolishly, while everyone complained to each other, no-one confronted the culprit. We had given him an inch, and now he would take the yard, along with our peace and quiet.

I grew up in the sixties when music was king, but it was not a dictator. Of course we were limited to vinyl and analogue radio, both of which had a fixed volume control. In addition these innovations were limited to the length of an extension lead, or convenience of transportation. The comical image of the scarcely portable ghetto blasters, or boom boxes, were still in the 1980s future.

Neither were we cursed with intrusive audio accompaniment which now follows us into the most intimate areas of our lives. The first wonderful miracle of mobile 'phones has now metamorphosed into all singing, all dancing, technological Frankensteins. Don't get me wrong all these are great inventions in their place, which, to my mind, is nowhere within my earshot.

Anyway, stepping off the soapbox, and back to our individual problem, which increased as the fine weather continued. What also grew was popular irritation with the situation.

Initially neighbours had attempted a personal approach, which was greeted with varying degrees of patronising contempt, or outright arrogance. Either way the result was the same: far from toning it down, music and voice levels increased a couple of notches. Later, various applications to the relevant authorities produced some temporary respite, but led to unpleasant retaliations. Vandalism and intimidating behaviour which could not be legally substantiated. The community divided between fear and feigned apathy.

Eventually all methods, short of a twelve bore, had been exhausted. Well perhaps not quite.

During all this farce of fruitless negotiations and failures I had already foreseen the frustrating outcome. Instead of wasting effort, and making myself prominent, I thought long and hard about the problem and came up with a solution. The beauty of the idea was that I had everything I needed to inflict the most exquisitely apt punishment. Even more ironic, the offender had helpfully sown the seeds of his own retribution. I just needed to provide the fertiliser.

But this event would mark a milestone in my new vocation. To date I had fallen into my nemesis incarnation by an accident of fate. Now I would have to plan with all the meticulous detail and precision of a military campaign. This would be my first truly premeditated crime.

The crucial success of my strategy depended on the weather. So while others welcomed the merciful rain from heaven, I waited with the impatience of D Day generals for the sun. My feelings were mixed. On one hand, relief that my services may not be needed. On the other, disappointment to be thwarted and denied satisfaction.

In desperation I even took to listening to forecasts from the Met Office, which proved an exasperating waste of time. I was just debating whether a lump of seaweed may prove more accurate, when one morning in late August I awoke to dry pavements. I anxiously watched all morning until the remaining clouds floated away leaving an unblemished blue sky. But I wasn't until I heard the telltale sounds of that dreaded tedious pounding I knew it was "game on".

I went back inside, collected and checked my equipment, then waited. I had killed so much time already another few hours would pass easily enough. Besides I could use the time to mentally rehearse my mission. Once satisfied with that, I even had the unusual opportunity to analyse my emotions. If I had thought all the preparation and suspense would make me anxious, then I was wrong. I felt only increased excitement. The sort of thrill which comes with eager anticipation rather than nerves.

The rest of the day some mediocre television supplied one distraction, while the half hearted preparation of a Welsh rarebit provided another. My preoccupied mind had little interest in food, but my digestive system was so empty I was beginning to feel nauseous. So I ate a hearty supper, and then I watched the sky change from blue to black. Perfect: a new moon tonight, providing only faint illumination. Now I had only to avoid the less forgiving glare of neighbours' security lights.

My own bedroom light I left on: partly as a visual alibi but also a homing beacon. Then I put on my new black coat and shoved the kit into its deep pockets. Finally I pulled on some plastic disposable gloves and set off into the dark garden.

It took me, what seemed like hours, to negotiate my way through the assault course which made up my neighbours' gardens. A perilous business which involved avoiding vigilant dogs, startling prowling cats and, in one instance, causing panic to a neighbour's chickens as I passed their coop.

By the time I reached the objective my adrenaline was high and so, apparently, were all the members of the party. If my nasal senses did not deceive me, alcohol had not been the only refreshment on offer. Now I had a new concern: what if my target was not alone crashing out in the garden tonight. At the moment there appeared no likelihood of a mass exit, so I settled down in the refuge of the undergrowth and watched. I found myself fascinated by this rag tag collection of humanity, and passed the time studying their behaviour. They were an equal mix of gender and race but the release of their inhibitions had not led to an orgy.

It was more like watching the antics of a group of young children who had got at the cooking sherry. If only my intimidated neighbours could see their tormentors in this state! Almost before this thought developed into another the party was suddenly dissolving. One by one the guests went back into the house, mumbling some indecipherable babble, but did not return. Their host replied, in the same unintelligible vein, but could only physically manage the flick of a hand, which I took to serve as a goodbye wave. Then all that remained was a solitary shadowy outline, just visible against the dying charcoal embers. I continued my vigil a little longer, until darkness enclosed us both; stalker and prey.

Sometime later I arrived back home guided by my bedroom light. I climbed the stairs and threw the switch, plunging the house into darkness. Then I undressed, inserted some earplugs and dropped into the welcoming arms of Orpheus. No energetic sheep were required.

I awoke late the next day. Unusually for me, dawn had failed to interrupt my slumber. Once I vaguely remember partial awakening, but turned my back to the windows and rejoined oblivion. It was a Sunday morning so there was little movement or sound from the street to disturb me, even without the plugs. It was almost lunch time before I finally dragged my still hazy senses back into the land of the living. It took a few minutes more of quiet reflection before my body followed suit.

It was promising to be another warm day and as I opened the back door I heard voices. My neighbours engaged in their usual over the fence chitchat. Today, though, instead of the normal conversational tone their dialogue was louder, more animated and interspersed with exclamations of disbelief and laughter! I caught some of the gist: enough to confirm that my night's excursion was the cause of all this babble and mirth.

I could scarcely insert myself into a conversation held through the shrubbery and over several gardens. Such an action would have been out of character, if not outright suspicious. So I waited until a reasonable need for a forgotten grocery drove me out to our local convenience corner shop. As I guessed, there the main topic was the somewhat bizarre incidents of the previous night.

I assumed my best supporting actor role and prepared to give the performance of a lifetime.

The chain of events apparently went something like this. Shortly after I took the wise precaution of putting on some ear defenders an uproar shook the neighbourhood. However since this issued from vicinity of the notorious tenant's garden this did not immediately cause undue concern. I had hoped for this "crying wolf" response.

It took a good fifteen minutes before his nearest neighbours managed to liase and agreed to call the authorities. Direct intervention was quickly ruled out: given his previous history of harassment and following police advice. No, as usual, the commotion would have to be tolerated until the arrival of the noise control officer. Unfortunately this was likely to be later rather than sooner, since on a fine Saturday night his services would be in high demand.

This besieged official eventually arrived some half an hour later, by which time most of the disturbed neighbours had followed my lead with ear plugs. Luckily, because of the ongoing situation, most of them had acquired these useful devices. It took a further five minutes of investigation to discover that the premises were secured from the front. Another five to gain access from an adjoining garden. What the man discovered next was the cause of all this lively "morning after" post mortem.

Someone had managed to secure the substance sedated "victims" hands behind his back with plastic ties. The assailant had then applied copious amounts of super glue to the relevant components of an old type of personal stereo radio. The foam speakers were literally stuck into his ears, while the unit itself was found wedged in a very curious location. The "rescuer" only found it at all because, unable to remove the earpieces, he had followed the trailing wire to try and turn off the machine at source. There, nestling between the builder's crack, was a thankfully small Walkman. Before securing the unit the perpetrator had set the tuner to a classical station and turned the volume up full blast. I reflected that it had been an unpleasant job, but someone had to do it.

Despite the intrusive indignities already inflicted on his person, it wasn't until this final act that he was jolted to his remaining senses. You would, indeed, need to be stone deaf or brain dead not to react to the spirited rendition of the 1812 Overture plainly audible to the bewildered onlookers.

Even with his best efforts the noise control officer could not extricate either giver or receiver unit from the man's anatomy. Neither, given the position of the switches, could he reach the volume or on/off buttons. He conceded defeat and called the paramedics. By the time they arrived their patient was becoming frantic. They would have administered a tranquillizer but for the unknown mixture of drugs already consumed. The ambulance team had dealt with the effects of super glue before and decided to transfer their patient and the problem to the nearest A & E.

He was bundled into the emergency transportation to the astonishment of a rapidly growing crowd and the accompaniment of a more pianissimo piece. There followed a brief debate whether this was Mozart or Chopin.

The ordeal was nearly at an end – well at least for the neighbourhood. It took a little longer for the hospital staff to remove the offending instrument. They went for the easier option first: the choice not involving sensitive human flesh. Sensibly they loosened the glued in plug socket for the headphones and released the connection, thereby securing silence. Strangely no one thought of simply cutting the connecting wire!

It took a great deal more effort and discomfort to disentangle the patient. Subsequent tests revealed that although his hearing was damaged it was hoped to be a temporary injury. I had never foreseen this outcome: believing that someone would curtail the concert with a pair of scissors. But I sadly overestimated the human capacity for logic when under pressure.

I am afraid that my planned introduction to the joys of classical music had gone awry.

While the physical trauma was unpredicted and unintentional, the psychological effects were exactly as desired. This was obvious when he returned home the next day, clutching an appointment card for the ENT outpatients clinic. I did briefly consider that my actions might escalate more retaliation, but dismissed this. The youth was a bully and bullies traditionally retreat when confronted by a show of strength. This was exactly the case. He crept back into his hole with his tail – a rather tender one – between his legs.

Full details of his humiliation had spread the

neighbourhood like wildfire. Unlike most gossip it didn't even need the usual embroidery: the facts were hilarious enough. Perhaps a sad comment on human nature but not one person felt sorry for him. Well actually I felt a little guilty, but only for a short time. The time it took me to remember the misery he and his friends had inflicted on our innocent community. The balance had changed irrevocably. People began to wonder how they could possibly have been intimidated by him in the first place. Rather like the advice to imagine someone in authority naked, no one could erase the image of his embarrassing predicament

The architect of his downfall was a subject for much lively speculation and a cause for paranoia on the focus of all this unwanted attention. Even to the point that suspicion fell on his own circle of friends. It was this doubt which caused the only disruption to the calm which had returned to the neighbourhood. A very brief lapse when shouting could be heard drifting across the gardens, but with none of the usual musical enhancement. In fact music was now only noticeable by its absence.In this instance no one reached for a 'phone: everyone was too busy eavesdropping. The confrontation ended with the slamming of car doors and revving of engines.

Now utterly alienated, both from his cohorts and the neighbours who would have been his friends, the tenant kept a low profile. The shame could never be eradicated. The memory, and hopefully, lesson would follow him the rest of his life. Even when the whispering ceased, the curious looks remained. Even a well meaning smile was interpreted as a knowing smirk specifically calculated to torment him. While he remained he could not escape his notoriety. I have to confess that for a while I had brief misgivings that he may be next discovered in a worst, more terminal, condition. But no, suicide was not in his nature, so escape was his only option. Shortly afterwards he abandoned his lease and departed – a sadder and wiser man.

I was glad: he was a selfish moron, but he did not deserve to pay the ultimate price.

Life settled back to its former routine, but the story lived on in the realms of local folklore. In doing so it gained a sort of timeless status usually reserved for morality lessons or urban legends. It became an anecdote passed on between families and friends whenever a dark mood required lifting.

In due course the property was reoccupied. Everyone held their breath and strained their ears, ready to intervene at the first hint of noise. It never came. The new resident was a student, but a rare specimen whose major was education, not alcohol. While memories are long, hope springs eternal. All the barriers came down and the young man quickly became a welcome asset rather than a potential threat.

The Summer continued on into September. Autumn arrived with such gentleness that we hardly noticed the shortened days and cooler nights. Then one morning the leaves were suddenly transformed into that breathtaking array of colours which is their final declaration of life.

Autumn was never my favourite season, much preferring the assurance of Spring. But age has mellowed me, and given me a fresh appreciation of its qualities. Perhaps it is merely that with my advancing years I have found a mutual empathy. The example nature provides is not to be content with growing old gracefully but to do so with joyous spectacle. Both seasons share many similarities. Not least because despite being often fleeting, they are incredibly productive. They give a real sense of the cycle of life which the stagnant seasons of summer and winter do not. It is therefore probably no accident that we humans catch this fever. Spring actually gives its name to this phenomena. It is a common belief that pregnant women suddenly begin cleaning house as birth is imminent. In common with nesting birds and animals it is perhaps a preparation to welcome new life.

Towards the end of the year its older cousin is similarly busy. Autumn begins clearing up ready for the long winter and we once more follow suit. Even in ancient days it was a time for celebration. Now the pagan revels are channelled into harvest festivals and annual street fairs.

As for me, well I had my own house keeping, and part of this involved a final trip to Wales.

Chapter Seven

A FARMER'S TALE

Just as my first visit to Wales in June was to open up the caravan; my last journey was to secure it for the winter. So, around the end of October, before the first significant frosts could damage its delicate plumbing, I loaded up the car and headed north west.

Over the summer I had made several identical trips: all of which were uneventful, and none of which incorporated an en route stop at the notorious service station. The expeditions shared another ingredient: they were all of, at least, a week's duration. The minimum five hour driving experience generally precluded any shorter stay: a couple of nights relaxation would hardly be worth the stress.

In this instance I took the opportunity to mix necessity with pleasure. We were currently enjoying the benefits of an Indian Summer and I was determined to make the most of this rare phenomena. Winter would soon be closing the door on most outdoor activities, so, between chores, I explored some of the roads less travelled.

It was on one of these excursions that I found myself on a single track road, with worryingly few passing places. I was alternating between creeping around blind bends, and pushing the throttle on open straights, when a dog ran across my path. Luckily for us both I was braking into a corner when the incident happened. I had time to register, with relief, that the animal escaped unscathed. As I saw it disappear into the hedgerow I also noted it was a popular breed for those parts, a border collie. However it was a sad example: even through its thick matted coat you could distinguish bone rather than substantial flesh. It seemed fit enough though. As I paused it emerged into the field and then bounded away up an hillside.

I resumed my journey, which only lasted a few more minutes before the first sign of civilisation appeared. One of the more traditional and timeless visions of rural life: the village pub. Although sadly nowadays, increasingly, even their names have lost any sense of individuality. Many have been devoured by the insatiable and expensive "gastro" trend, which is generally advertised by a depressing nondescript two tone signage. This understatement is somehow considered to be attractive and denote excellence. No doubt there are some excellent restaurants hiding beneath this blanket. All too often it just signifies portions reminiscent of the dreaded "nuvo cuisine" and a price list requiring a loan application.

Inns conventionally used to greet the weary traveller, but now they seem, blatantly, to focus on their wallets. In my, admittedly, limited experience "welcome" is the last thing on many of the owners' minds.

I was relieved to see that this isolated specimen, with its hand painted sign, appeared to have escaped this sorry fate. It may look a little neglected around the edges, perhaps needing a fresh coat of paint, but it had one important feature. "Character" is a rare quality, whether in buildings or people. It cannot be taught, it can only be experienced. And, at this moment, following my recent jolt, I wanted its comforting familiarity. For that I would willingly sacrifice a superior dining experience.

As I indicated and turned into the car park I had no difficulty in imagining that I was following in the tracks of so many generations of horse drawn and horseless carriages.

I was not disappointed by the interior, it matched its advertisement perfectly. I had not been mis-sold: this was an honest village local, not a wannabe gourmet restaurant/bar. This was the real thing: original oak beams and furniture, instead of pine imports. Horse brasses and general agricultural bric a brac decorated the walls, without a wine bottle in sight. All of this gave me the stability I craved, even before a jovial landlord put in his appearance. I selected a good honest British fare of shepherd's pie, with a fruit juice accompaniment. My brief conversation with "mine host" took in my traumatic near miss. He replied by explaining that this must be "Sam", a frequent escapee from a well known local farmer.

While waiting for the order I scanned the room for a suitable table. My fellow clientele were all locals, except for an elderly couple. No doubt the tourists who owned the camper van outside. I noted a small window seat was vacant and took up residence.

As with small communities the atmosphere was lively but lacking variety. My exchange with the landlord had, of course, been overheard and provided a welcome diversion. A spirited debate commenced about the merits, or rather lack of them, regarding their absent neighbour.

Apparently the man lived alone on a small farm about a mile away. A bit of a recluse he was seldom seen except to curse at locals and tourists alike. As the conversation grew more animated so did the contributions of the participants. Rumour had it that there had been a spouse at some point in his history, who had been witnessed in the village shop cum post office. But her visits had ceased some years since: she had no doubt seen the error of her ways and absconded to the bright lights of some city.

There then followed a discussion on the consequences of the horrific outbreak of foot and mouth which had led to the destruction of all local livestock. This carnage included the unsociable shepherd's flock. For any other farmer this tragedy would have only brought sympathy from his fellow sufferers, but misfortune had only made a bad nature worse. Besides which he had apparently found another more lucrative, and less hazardous, venture which brought only disgust from the assembled group.

Hardened to cruel reality as farmers must inevitably become, even they were appalled by his new enterprise. Whereas he had initially chosen his solitary lifestyle, he now had no choice in the matter. There are some activities which test the bounds of decency, and even to these cynical men puppy farming was one. The fact that he seemed to relish the suffering inflicted by this occupation put him beyond the pale of his community.

Many people draw an imaginary line between the ill treatment of animals and human beings. I hold no such demarcation for cruelty. In fact I consider the abuse of any weaker creature, be it two, four legged, or indeed without legs at all, beyond forgiveness. Such sadists, whether they lurk in farms, laboratories or hospitals, to my mind, have no conscience. If they had they could not bear to live with themselves.

My only knowledge of puppy farms had been through the sanitized exposure documentaries on tv. Even those I have barely managed to endure to conclusion, and none without leaving a permanent mark. I call it my "Bambi" complex.

As a child my grandfather mistakenly took me to see the film – believing it was a harmless cartoon. The upshot was that within a very short space of time he found a distraught grand daughter on his hands, whom he could only begin to pacify by escorting her from the cinema. The lesson stayed with me for ever, to the point that I seldom watch any films where animals play a significant part.

It was not therefore with any pleasure that when I left the pub I headed in the direction described by my lunch companions. Despite this reluctance injustice drew me like a magnet. I could no more avoid this course than I could block the blessing and curse of an overactive imagination.

I drove slowly along a sign less road, on which the asphalt eventually degraded to dirt. Civilisation, even with its flaws, was being left behind, and I felt anxious. My vehicle was now completely off the beatentrack, one which I suspected had never received any Department of Transport designation. But I had help in the form of my constant travel companion: a road map which included ordnance survey details.

The latter marked all buildings of interest – including farms. I had followed the silent navigator on my passenger seat: stopping at junctions for guidance. The latest fork had brought me close to the tiny symbol, but surrounded by a dense overgrowth of bushes and trees, I could see no man made structure.

There was a chill in the air, but perhaps nerves had caused a belated hot flush, because I wound down the window. With no isolating glass I now received my first hint of some form of life: the muffled, but unmistakeable noise of dogs. Not the annoying, but healthy, sound of barking, but many throats howling or whimpering. Sounds of distress.

I reluctantly left the safety of the car, automatically locking it behind me. The keys I slipped between the fingers of my right hand: a sort of impromptu knuckleduster I had learnt about some time ago during a self defence session.

A concealed gap appeared to my left and I steeled myself as I rounded a bend and almost ran into a farm gate concealed by a badly neglected hedge. The remnants of a farm came into view, which temporarily stopped me in my tracks. I paused waiting to decide my next move when a large, in every sense, figure emerged from one of many ramshackle outbuildings. This colossus looked threatening enough, without the shotgun he carried.

I stood my ground, I had no option. The "man" had already spotted me. While a confrontation was unpleasant, the alternative of retreat and thus exposing my back was unthinkable.

Summoning up all my willpower, and suppressing every survival instinct, I approached the gate. He, likewise, moved forwards and we stood facing each other like some bizarre parody of a Wild West gunfight. His voice, however, dispelled the comparison. He had a strong accent. It is usually a pleasure to hear the soft lyrical dialect, but any enjoyment was spoilt by the harsh tone. As we stared at each other across the barred gate I was mollified to see that the gun was broken in safety mode.

I interpreted from his grunts that he wanted to know my business. More by intuition than intention, I truthfully explained the incident with his dog. This animal was even now cowering behind its ungrateful master. I had driven up here with no plan, but unexpectedly inspiration came to me. There was one consideration which would advance my cause – greed. So I offered to buy his dog.

At the mention of money his expression changed from suspicion to a peculiar combination of cunning and something resembling a smile, which I took to be wind. The very malevolence of that look made me feel contaminated. I suddenly had an overpowering urge to step into a refreshing shower. All I wanted to do was get out of there as soon as possible.

Instead I stood my ground and went into full BS mode. I could see the avaricious circuits turning on full strength in his brain. He had another proposition in mind. He suggested that perhaps I would prefer a younger companion and offered to show me a selection. This was the last thing on earth I wanted to see. But he invited me inside by opening the gate, and caught in my own web, I walked in.

I grudgingly followed my guide towards the plaintive sounds which had been continuing throughout our exchange. We entered the largest building and what I can only describe as a canine battery farming establishment.

Stacked cages lined the walls where the adult mothers lived out their miserable lives of relentless birth and death in the twilight provided by broken boards in the walls and roof. It was an earthly Hell with worse scents than the sulphur normally associated with those dark regions. For a animal lover it was beyond adequate description. How I did not kill him then and there astonishes me at my own willpower.

With a monumental effort I resumed my role, which helped disguise the sickening disgust. As a potential client I declined his offer, saying thatI had decided after all not to buy a pet. I avoided his face, which I knew would be made foul by his anger and frustration. I departed as quickly as possible, with one backward regretful glance in my rear view mirror. I hoped that he would not take out his mercenary disappointment on the pathetic dog still standing nearby. But, thankfully, wisely out of kicking range.

I would have taken the collie away, but a plan was already forming, and I could not risk a distraction for one life when I intended to save many. The dog had survived so long, perhaps he could hold out just a little longer – I really hoped so.

But time was now of critical importance. I would have to be quick. Perhaps I had aroused the brute's suspicions, if so self preservation could well surpass greed. There was no doubt about his lack of compassion, or abundance of opportunity, to "dispose" of any living evidence. In fact I had already noticed a possible method in the farm yard.

If I had been a cartoon character this was the moment a light bulb would have appeared above my head! I began my plan at its conclusion and worked backwards to its starting point. The experience with the neighbour from Hell would now prove a useful rehearsal of my organisational skills. In fact very little preparation was required: just the time and cost of two 'phone calls. Both made at local public booths: I knew that mobiles were more vulnerable to detection. Now I was ready, but had to await a certain set of circumstances.

Firstly it was crucial that a witness could provide proof that the farmer was seen alive after my visit to the pub. As far as I knew no-one was aware of my detour to the farm, but I wanted to be sure my appearance was not linked with his disappearance

I had overheard enough conversation to know that his only contact with the village was a weekly visit to reclaim his mail from the post office. It was observed that this always coincided with early closing day: Wednesday. A cause of exasperation to the post mistress since he always turned up a few minutes before noon, but then dawdled around until at least half an hour had eaten into her free time.

It was now Monday, so I had just two days to wait. Two days which crept by, although I tried to fill them with physical distraction. The caravan never looked so clean: it sparkled inside and out. I had the consolation that this was not a useless exercise. For one thing, it served to provide an exhausted night's sleep. For another it was essential preparation for my swift departure.

There was a second component to my plan and I mentally crossed all fingers and toes that the weather would remain dry. I had learnt a lesson from the service station fiasco – the importance of "covering my tracks". Just to be sure I kept a pair of outsized Wellingtons in the car. Although, if events went as intended, distinguishing my presence at this crime scene would be like looking for a tree in a forest.

Wednesday. Everything was now ready. All I awaited was my most dependable ally: darkness. The nights had drawn in so much that evening had altogether vanished. My unwitting conspirator was providing a twelve hour slot of opportunity, of which I would take full advantage.

By 6pm I had loaded up the car, double checked the caravan, and sealed it for the winter. The site owners would, at a small fee, drain down the pipes later. I did not see anyone as I drove away. Not surprising: given the time of year and day of week. The small park was deserted.

Not even a surveillance camera witnessed my departure. It would hardly matter if they did: in fact it may even provide an alibi in the event of any later enquiries.

My first destination was a previously recced public phone box: conveniently situated in a poorly lit lane. From there I made my first anonymous call of the evening. The wheels were set in motion.

I did likewise with my car and headed back to the farm. This time I had researched a more circuitous route bypassing the nearby village. Everything looked so different in the dark. My decision to drive solely on sidelights added to the confusion. But I had all night – or rather a good part of it – so I erred on the side of caution and crawled around the meandering lanes.

The only landmarks I could remember were natural ones, mainly large significant trees. One of these, an ancient oak, I recalled from my last visit. It was easily distinguishable, even in this gloom, from its distinctive outline against the moon lit sky. I parked up under its wide canopy, grabbed my torch and continued on foot along the rutted track. Everything else I needed was stuffed in my ample coat pockets. The possible residue of my tyre marks did not concern me – one specific vehicle would make very little difference to the general chaos this night.

It took less than ten minutes to reach the approach to the farm. Almost as soon as I recognised the gate I heard a piteous whine. All caution abandoned, and with adrenaline pumping, I cleared the gate with aplomb worthy of Red Rum.

Even in my haste I stooped, zigzagging my way across the open yard, using derelict machinery for cover. I followed the heartbreaking cry towards the farm house, all the while alert for signs of the owner. There was a faint light in the property, which by its flickering could be coming from a television screen. But I clung to the shadows, straining my eyes against the darkness – searching for my old friend – hoping he was still safe.

I was halfway towards the dwelling when suddenly the door was flung open and a huge shape appeared silhouetted against a dim light from the tilley lamp he carried. He was shouting curses which were almost incoherent through his rage and strong dialect. He stormed to his right and I heard a heart rending yelp as a successfully aimed kick connected.

I clenched impatient fists as I watched the monster walk back towards the house, holding my breath and temper until he disappeared inside. Then I moved quickly towards the whimpering dog. I reached forward, stretching out my hand until I felt something gently accepting the offering I held out. I imagine the poor creature had never smelt, let alone tasted, steak in his cheerless life. I gently untied the rough rope and replaced it with a collar and lead, all the while talking soothingly. Affection was something else he had probably never experienced, because he followed like a lamb.

With kindness and best sirloin I think he would have come with me to the ends of the earth. As it was I only required companionship for a short, but precarious distance, to an area I had noticed on my earlier visit.

We moved side by side, very gradually, towards my objective. When I estimated we were in its general vicinity I risked confirmation with a quick flash of my torch. Yes, we just needed to move a little more to the left.

When I was certain of my bearings, I took up position and put the second part of my plan into operation. The torch I stowed away in one of my seemingly bottomless pockets. There was enough natural light for what I needed – in fact pitch black would be ideal.

I have always believed in travelling light, the more so as I have grown older where time has become less infinite, and therefore more precious. My plans were turning out to be no different, requiring only a small stash of equipment: torch, steak, dog lead and whistle. I removed the latter from my pocket and blew as hard as I could.

I didn't wait long for results. From the barn and my heels came the almost joyous sound of barking. Joyous, because despite having all pleasure in life denied them, the dogs were still able to return to their natural state. At least the bastard, unlike many laboratories, had been too miserly to remove their voice boxes. Or perhaps he was just unable to find a vet who would agree to this obscene mutilation. And we call animals savage!

Accompanying this uproar of noise I saw an oblong of light as the house door once more flew open. A familiar large shape temporarily blocked most of this illumination while I watched events unfold.

As I hoped he came straight for his usual punch bag: obviously believing that the dog had slipped his tether. He had replaced the tilley with a modern torch and I saw the beam flashing an arc as he scanned the yard for the delinquent collie. The dog played his part to perfection and was by now in a barking frenzy. I had tied him safely to a old fence post and left him. Of course deprived of his new best friend and treats he forgot all the fear beaten into him, and howled for all he was worth.

I had badly mistimed how fast such a leviathan could shift andconsequently almost collided with him as we both moved in opposing directions. But his mind was on other things, like giving his dog another undeserved thrashing. So it was easy to sidestep him and he rushed passed me. The movement though disorientated me, and he had almost reached the dog before I recovered.

I was soon in no doubt that this was intended as a final solution when I saw the metal poker he held in his hand. He was just a few yards from the animal when I saw him raise the weapon, with every intention of destroying his "pet".

Several feet now separated me from the bully, but it was proving to be the night for dormant athletic achievement. I covered the distance easily by a spectacular dive. If I say so myself it was an incredible feat for a sexagenarian.

I made contact low on his ample hips and this, combined with the upward movement of his arms, threw him off balance. My elaborate plans could not have worked better than my forced improvisation. I dived inelegantly, but landed lightly on to the ground: thanking my genes that osteoporosis does not run in my family.

Meanwhile my opponent abandoned everything in an

effort to save himself. The torch disappeared first, throwing us all into darkness, where the poker ended up I had no idea. Seconds later I heard the sound of a splash and realised that something had fallen foul of the slurry pit. This was the area I had noticed on my first visit and later formed the crucial ingredient of my scheme. The dog, I was relieved to hear, continued his accompaniment from safety.

The bigger they come the harder they fall. The proof of this proverb was being demonstrated even as I staggered to my feet. Ahead of me in the darkness came unmistakeable noises of a desperate struggle. A mixture of gurgled cries and a strange burbling, "sucking" sound. The disturbing intensity of the situation was magnified by my temporary loss of vision. It is a well known fact, exploited by all makers of the horror film genre, that the most primitive human fears are stimulated by the dark. In the shadows lurk unknown terrors more terrible than any reality, and only limited by our imaginations. As for my own imagination – well that is healthy enough to fill a lifetime of nightmares. Reality, I decided, could be no worse. So I fumbled around and retrieved my torch. My first priority was the dog, so following the beam, I found my way back to him. Our reunion immediately silenced him, but, to be certain, I offered another chunk of steak.

I then swung my torch in the direction of the man made swamp. The cries had ceased: all I could detect was a weird squelching sound. It took me a couple of passes across the black surface to spot anything at all. Then the shaft of light picked out the reflection of two small white dots. For a split second my brain could not compute what my eyes were seeing. But that was it exactly – eyes. What I saw resembled some extinct primeval creature, barely recognisable as any living species.

The impact from our collision had carried him into the middle of the foul, pungent mire. He was now almost completely absorbed into the bog, only his head remained visible. He had ceased shouting because he vainly hoped to avoid inhaling the toxic liquid. It is poignant that, in moments of approaching death, common sense is obscured by hope, and we would sell our souls for just one more breath.

He must have known that I could not rescue him, even if I wanted to – I did not want to.

There was one fleeting moment of pity, but this was eclipsed by a thought which sank compassion quicker than his descent into the pit. It was the reflection that this was probably the fate for his animals once ill health or age made them surplus to requirements. It was therefore only kismet that he should join them in their putrid watery grave.

I glanced down at the collie and knew that, but for my intervention, he would be out there in that wretched Hell. The last vestige of sympathy fell away and I took satisfaction in the knowledge that his last sight on earth would be one of the creatures he so badly mistreated. I doubt if he would have time to appreciate the irony.

Cold blooded perhaps, but not so heartless as his treatment of other weaker species. I have never harmed any animal or child, nor could envisage any circumstance which would bring this about. Another way I do not fit the typical serial killer stereotype,

Rough justice, maybe, but nevertheless in the best biblical, Old Testament tradition. An eye for an eye. Not exactly like for like, but I think suffocating in animal excrement was a fitting punishment for their torture.

When he had vanished and the slurry settled, I untied the collie and, we took a leisurely walk back to my vehicle. En route I snubbed my toe on some unyielding object, and realised I had found the poker. It joined its owner, where it would never poke a fire, or murder a dog again.

Animals are not at all dumb in any sense of the word, and my companion was happy to jump onto the seat as I opened the car door. We exchanged a brief look before I started the engine, and I swear I saw more intelligence in those brown trusting eyes than most of my previous passengers. I like to believe he understood why I was leaving his friends behind.

I had a final task to perform on the long journey south. For this I made one more stop: at a garage where we could both take a toilet break and I found an old, but operative, phone booth.

I redialled the number I had keyed in earlier. The same voice answered and I gave the awaited response. This consisted basically of the truth: my reconnaissance of the farm and confirmation of its vile trade. I provided a brief description of the area and ended with a warning about the dangers of a slurry pit.

I did not mention its new resident, just that I had watched the farmer leave. This was not a lie: I just neglected to elaborate that when he departed it was not his premises, but life. I then replaced the receiver.

The number I disconnected was leftover from another lifetime, when I worked in publishing.

It was while researching illustrations for an animal rights

book that I came across a photographer who infiltrated laboratories and slaughter houses to reveal inhumane practices which would turn most of us vegetarian. We may be natural carnivores but in practice most of us are hypocritical ones. Unlike our ancestors we no longer have to kill to eat flesh: we seldom even have to think about its origins. While I prefer vegetables to meat I am still as guilty as anyone of this cowardice.

It is bravery on a whole different level which is willing to undergo greatpersonal trauma to bring cruelty to the public attention. I had a brief taste of this when I entered that stinking barn. If I had to endure that level of emotional distress on a regular basis, I would not vouch for my sanity.

This female photographer, who I was proud to call my friend, was truly amazing. Not only had she managed to avoid psychiatric treatment, but she retained a incredible sense of humour. She had one other valuable asset: she knew several equally dedicated friends and one of these possessed the number I had just rung.

As I drove back out into the night I knew that elsewhere other drivers and vehicles would be doing exactly the same thing. My early start had ensued that a good eight hours remained for their rescue operation.

As I said I am a reasonable mimic and used a west midlands accent for the call. I knew, before hanging up, that all the animals would be safely removed before dawn. I had no fear of endangering anyone: for one thing it may be a while before the farmer surfaced, if ever.

There was no sign of violence on his body, even if police dredged the pit, and accident was the probable verdict. In addition it would be next to impossible to prove any ill doing on the part of the animal rights group, or indeed identify them. No, I was convinced of their safety. They were professionals and would make sure that they left no evidence to tie them to the raid, let alone link them to the demise of the owner.

With the group's links around the country, very soon all the evidence (the parents and puppies) would be dispersed to all points of the UK compass. For the first times in their hitherto miserable lives they would be settling into real homes. Safely absorbed into families who would protect rather than exploit them. There only remained one outstanding problem.

This I had chosen to bring home with me. My first action was to give him a name: Lucky. Not a very original christening I'll agree, but he seemed to like it.

He was no trouble, being brought up in the school of hard knocks, he was docile and eager to please. Dogs require very little from an owner, which is probably just as well because all too often they receive much less. To friends and neighbours I explained that I had found him as a stray wandering loose around a motorway service station. The dumped victim of a callous owner long gone. He would have made a great pet, but unfortunately Lucky had yet to find his permanent home.

I would have kept him, but given the hazardous nature of my own life choices, I could not risk putting the neglected animal through more upheaval. If justice eventually caught up with me, who could say what would happen to him. But providence provided a solution. A good friend had recently "lost" her own elderly dog and was delighted to take over my charge.

It was with genuine sadness that I said my goodbyes. I like to think that he understood my motives, I knew he held no animosity: dogs rarely do. In fact they are often ridiculed for their unswerving loyalty, even in the face of extreme brutality. In doing this people make the mistake of interpreting trust as stupidity. Dogs are probably one of the most intelligent species (including homo sapiens) but unlike us they seldom losetheir belief in goodness. When we force them against their nature the results are dangerous to both parties.

Lucky had not yet reached this point and now had every chance of rebuilding that damaged faith. I watched as they drove off and he held his vigil at the back window until it turned the corner and disappeared.

Chapter Eight

THE VICAR'S TALE

By the time Lucky left Christmas had arrived.

We had been through the usual mayhem of holidays which signal the metamorphosis of autumn into winter. At this time of year celebrations follow each other – almost as quickly as the shelf changes in the shops.

So it is that before the remnants of picnic and barbeque paraphernalia are cleared away, the stores and supermarkets are stocking up with sweets and all manner of suitably ghoulish accessories. Summer dresses and beach wear are supplanted on clothes hangers by a diverse range of fancy dress costumes. Most of which seem to have absolutely no connection with the spirit (excuse pun) of Halloween at all.

I mean being greeted on the doorstep by, seemingly, the entire cast of Scooby-Doo is bewildering, but at least appropriate. Whereas the combination of a pirate, penguin, and princess, even with a token pumpkin, is just plain weird.

All Hallows Eve is another festival transformed from original pagan roots, one being the ancient Celtic Samhain. On this night, it is said, ghosts, and other supernatural beings, are released from the Other World to briefly rejoin us. Thanks to the good old U.S. of A this sinister carnival has been transformed into the jovial practice of the "Trick or Treat." Although I have still to be convinced that being visited by groups of bizarrely attired youngsters intent on blackmail is actually an improvement. No sooner do we breathe a sigh of relief as the last "vampire" extracts their calorie loaded ransom, than any remaining peace is shattered. Bonfire Night has arrived.

Remember, remember the fifth of November
Gunpowder, treason and plot.
I see no reason, why gunpowder treason
Should ever be forgot.

Since fireworks and their sale seem to continue from November into the New Year I don't see how there is any danger of forgetting – even if we wanted to. Believe me when I am startled into consciousness at midnight by a volley of explosions I really want to. Lack of sleep is a major test of self control, and the temptation for reprisal has been great. But you cannot kill someone for insomnia – or can you? You could probably legitimately forward a plea of temporary insanity.

Even worse, this is an opportunity for further extortion. This time there is no pretence of anything other than the acquisition of hard cash. A necessary conspirator to this felony is a representation of Guy Fawkes. Most of the time the "guy" is barely recognisable as anything except a bundle of rags with a mask tied to the region designated as his head. This flimsy dummy can usually be found propped against a wall to prevent total collapse.

No one nowadays seems to possess the skill or energy necessary to construct the traditional wooden cart for this effigy's transportation. Sometimes a discarded shopping trolley serves the purpose. They are the perfect modern substitute: easily accessible, requiring no manual labour, and most important of all – free.

To add insult to injury, we know that any "donations" we make to these pint sized con artists will be used against us. Although not generally acknowledged, such contributions have conventionally been intended to subsidise the purchase of fireworks.

In my own childhood fireworks were always fun, but then their enjoyment came from novelty. Nowadays there appears no limit to their exclusivity. Sometimes in the summer, always in the autumn, our ears are assaulted by a bombardment of noise. This veritable barrage is kept up regardless of day, even hour. By the end of the new year pyrotechnics, which signals a cease fire, many of us are suffering from shell shock.

We all have our crosses to bear, and just as we suffer the enforced excitement of Bonfire Night, our American "cousins" celebrate Thanksgiving. After all what you really really want just before Christmas is more turkey!

The only consolation is that Christmas on the other side of "the pond", despite its frenzied and lengthy build up, ends with the day. It is business as usual on 26th. On the other hand Christmas in the UK extends to merge with the New Year celebrations. Not that I am complaining, except so invariably do the leftovers.

All this manic activity at the end of the year, has always seemed to me, extremely bad planning. To cram so much into the last two months of the old year while leaving nothing for the first two months of the new is a recipe for disaster. It puts so much pressure on the importance of "enjoyment" that the holidays can become a matter of desperation.

Not so for me. Christmas is usually a quiet time, but never depressing. Without sounding like "thought for the day" it is a chance to relax and reflect. A few moments to pause and remember other Christmases: but not in a sad or remorseful way. The end of anything is like that: whether it is a relationship, job, life, or in this case, year. I suppose it's a way of stock taking: going back over past memories before creating future ones. Hoping perhaps to avoid the same mistakes: while knowing you are guaranteed to create new ones.

In my many years on this fragile planet I have never once made a New Year's resolution. Oh yes it's all very inspiring and "feel good" – for a day or so, but to me it's setting yourself up for a fall. It's right and natural to plan for the future, as long as you live for the present: one second at a time.

Christmas is just such an oasis. A point where you can slow down the clock to the point that it seems to stand still. Every moment can be savoured – if you stop worrying about tomorrow and how many different meals you can concoct with turkey remains. A bird of epic proportions, which has replaced the biblical loaves and fishes

Peace – so often the sentiment on greetings cards – but in reality a precious commodity over the holidays. It is traditionally a family time. Only right since it celebrates the first family, and I don't mean The White House. No, for those of you completely lost to the true meaning of Christ mass, I refer to Bethlehem.

Living alone I could be, and probably am, a subject of pity over the holidays, but I actually enjoy the peace. Sometimes I suspect there is a secret element of envy in this concern. How many mums and dads would love the luxury of falling asleep in a chair after the ordeal of Christmas lunch. There is no doubt that it is a desperate time for many solitary people, but I am not in that number.

I have no grandchildren, or even children, but if I require the more lively aspects of the season, then I have plenty of friends with energized offspring. Oddly enough the parents are more than happy to hand over their prized responsibilities for an hour, or three.

Despite my previous comments and contrary to your perception of me, Ido actually like children. It is refreshing to still find such offensive honesty. Unfortunately this only lasts a short while. The gap between natural candour and "monkey see, monkey do" is sadly too brief. In this case for "monkey" read parent. While preaching one set of morality, their behaviour often forms another. Leading by example into an emphasis on self and hypocrisy, rather than compassion and truth.

So, after two months of unwelcome doorstep visitors, it is almost a pleasure to be greeted by the final invaders of the year; carol singers. Sadly these are becoming increasingly rare, as are the once prolific nativity plays.

Many schools have abandoned this conventional Christian entertainment in favour of a more multi cultural approach. Unfortunately by this decision they often offend everyone and please no one. Whatever happened to tolerance and mutual respect?

You may think it odd, given my somewhat unorthodox

recent conduct, but I do like to celebrate Christmas for its true meaning – we are all hypocrites. Fortunately for me our local reformed church continues the tradition. Fortunately for them they have enough young children in the congregation to make this possible.

So, as my concession to the season of good will, I went along to this evening performance. It had all the dramatic components of tragedy and comedy: some encompassing both. Like when a distracted Joseph delivered the baby from its hiding place behind the manger and dropped it on its head. The new "mother" was suitably outraged: yanked the newborn from its "father," stuffed it in the crib, all the while giving her spouse G.B.H. of the ear hole. A prospective Oscar nominee could not have been more incensed, nor deserved the award more.

By the time the post performance mince pie and beverages arrived all the normal Anglo Saxon barriers were down. If laughter is the best medicine then we were all in the peak of health.

It was during this animated gathering that I learnt of a potential threat hanging over this small, but thriving congregation. There was little consolation in the fact that they were not alone in their fears.

Apparently there had been a spate of lead thefts in the area. This crime had mainly concerned church properties, and in fact had come close to devastating the very roof I stood under. Only last week an attempt had been foiled by fate in the shape of a passing late night cyclist.

Everyone seemed relieved and comforted by the fact that they would not return. My knowledge of criminal psychology however was not so optimistic.

In my work experience I remember once an incident where a burglary had led to the theft of all the company laptops. One week later they returned and removed all the desk tops and other valuable technological assets. It didn't end there. As soon as insurance had replaced all the devices the following night the culprits paid another visit and took all the substitutes.

I thought no more about it, just another irritation in life. That the victims should be churches did not surprise me. The practicalities mean that such large, old buildings are generally those which have this expensive metal commodity. They are also easy targets since most of the time they are uninhabited and therefore vulnerable.

Thieves are not the glamorous, almost heroic, characters of legend or literature. They are not Robin Hood, or even Raffles, they are opportunism cowards, who prey on the weak.

Christmas passed and we began again the long haul through bleak January, which this year lived up to its reputation. No snow, but endless bitterly cold wind and rain. This combination kept everyone indoors. At least the novelty of "the white stuff" brings a rush outside to the nearest slopes with any article capable of sitting or lying on. The more innovative, or pretentious, commuters grab their skis, which they seemingly keep in readiness by the front door. Every year these individuals are duly photographed and appear in the local and national news as evidence of "extreme" conditions.

However at the moment the weather confirmed met office predictions. The rain barrels overflowed, and the gales dislodged anything loose from the trees and roofs. To make matters worse, although the shortest day had come and gone, daylight hours refused to lengthen. We lived as enormous moles, and growing larger: too much food and too little exercise. There was no threat, or promise, of snow, so the landscape and skies were predominantly grey. Streets and parks remained deserted, except for the most committed joggers.

Everyone was getting gaol fever, but no one felt inclined to make an escape bid. For parents and children the daily school run was a miserable chore. While the rest of us confined our outdoors activities to the weekly shopping trip Both forms of excursions only grudgingly undertaken as unpleasant necessities.

Nothing broke the monotony. The only distance light on the horizon was the prospect of the next bevy of holidays. This would begin with St Valentine's Day, and continue through Mothering Sunday to the next major event – Easter. No surprise then that the local news was also going through a lean period. Apparently it was too desolate, even for crime. Although not quite true, since the dark nights provided perfect conditions for some nefarious, after hours, thievery. In short the lead strippers were back at work after a brief Christmas break.

It was their misfortune that this coincided with my own return to business. It had been a quiet time since my return from Wales, and this situation presented a challenge for my new found skills. Perhaps I was becoming some sort of adrenaline junkie, or maybe I was just bored. Whatever the reason, or combination of reasons, it spelled trouble for the robbers and deliverance for their intended victims.

Okay it would entail a few sleepless nights, but what else

had I to do during the day except catch up. Besides too much time provided the opportunity for thought and I needed diversion. It was too late for soul searching: if indeed I possessed such an elusive object. Nevertheless I still had a persistent conscience. Not with regard to the deceased, no avenging ghosts disturbed my slumbers or daydreams.

My ethical dilemma was more fundamental: was I justified in taking the law into my own hands? If I had a "God" complex how much easier life would become, but I did not, so doubts would occasionally surface.

These felons had no conscience, so I pushed my own aside. They targeted defenceless buildings and demoralized their congregations. People who were still valiantly attempting to live their lives by a 'turn the other cheek' philosophy in the face of a 'dog eat dog' society.

I am under no illusion that all Christians actually practice this virtue, but, for the most part, they try. Offering the other cheek may be very fine and dignified gesture, but I had another response in mind.

I had learnt from contacts at the church that Police estimated the time of the crimes between the hours of midnight and 3am. I also established that the church had installed no cameras or other security measures. They seemed to put all their faith in, what I considered, the erroneous belief that lightening never strikes twice.

Every night I donned on my camouflage gear and snuck out across the back gardens and through a derelict plot of land. Oddly enough my nocturnal ramblings always led to the same destination: the congregational church. This nightly foray would have been more stimulating, scary even, if it had been an ancient church, incorporating a graveyard.

But as I prowled around the secluded dark grounds, images of countless classic horror films came to mind. At these moments I was glad that no sinister monuments impeded my progress, or fed my imagination. It was all very well craving excitement from the security of daylight, but on the whole boredom was preferable. Besides I had the consolation that after so much physical apathy I badly needed the exercise.

I had plenty of that. It was almost the end of January, and I was beginning to doubt my conviction that the church would warrant a second assault. The temperatures were dropping into a more wintry region, and I was running out of thermal underwear, when my sleepless nights paid off.

I was keeping up my vigil, and avoiding frostbite by walking another circuit of the building. By now I knew its layout as well as that of my own home. Suddenly I heard the distinctive sound of a motor vehicle approaching. This event was not in itself unusual, and frequently gave me cause to halt my nightly constitutional.

But typically these disruptions came much earlier in the night and a quick glance at my watch confirmed the time as approaching 2am. The church had no immediate neighbour to account for this unsociable mid week disturbance, so I withdrew into the shadows of the surrounding bushes. As I waited I heard the engine die.

The sudden silence was quickly filled by voices, speaking in a language I did not understand. Now there are many hard working and decent migrants, but in every barrel there are rotten apples and sadly they always seem to rise to the top. Or rather they seem to provide the tabloids with suitably shocking headlines. I was both depressed and disappointed to learn that there was some basis for the newspaper reports.

I hardly had time to reflect on this development before I heard the distinctive scrape of metal against metal as the gates to the church grounds swung open. A few moments later I heard the crunch of the gravel drive as a large white van appeared in my line of sight. As it passed my hiding place it did so seemingly under its own volition. The driving seat was empty. However the reason became clear when the rear trundled into vision: two men were quietly pushing their getaway vehicle. I was grateful that, for their own security, they turned off the headlights because it protected mine.

I was also relieved that there were just two thieves: the prospect of dealing with a criminal gang had been a matter of concern. I continued to watch as one man secured the hand brake while the other refastened the gate. Obviously the need for secrecy outweighed that of a quick escape. Perhaps the open gate had been the downfall of their last attempt.

Once satisfied with their individual efforts, they teamed up to unload a large split ladder from the van's interior. It was an awkward manoeuvre, but it may have looked a trifle suspicious to be transporting such an item around the neighbourhood in plain sight. The van roof was therefore not an option.

Thank goodness they were obviously experts in their trade, because preliminaries didn't take long. It was becoming colder and I was rapidly turning into the churchyard's first monument. I could not even risk a quick foot stamp to resume blood circulation.

They were more confident than I, because I saw the

glow of a torch and from this wavering light I followed their movements. They must have been physically strong because the extended ladder was no easy burden. This fact gave me a few moments concern, but I was mollified to hear their grumbles and groans as the result of their efforts. They were merely human not supermen.

I followed along in the macabre procession. Fortunately moonlight shone in the right direction. I managed to move from the shadows of the foliage to those cast by the church without crossing a spot lit area. Now I regretted the fact that there was no gravestones to provide friendly cover.

They obviously remembered their previous access point, for, without hesitation, they headed straight for the lowest part of the roof. This was none the less still a good thirty feet high. I waited to see the next part of their strategy. I didn't wait long: they made short work of upending the ladder against the church wall. The first, larger, individual mounted first, carrying a rucksack, which no doubt contained the tools of his profession. A few seconds later he shouted down to his accomplice, who began climbing up after him.

This was good news for me. One flaw in my scheme, once the gang scenario was banished, was the possibility that one man would remain on the ground. No doubt they felt, given their former close shave, that time was of the essence and removing the lead required both pairs of hands. Another problem solved.

This was my chance and I seized it. The voices grew muted as they had moved away from the edge: no doubt checking their earlier abandoned handiwork. I rather hoped to prove the truth of one particular proverb – "what goes up must come down." I hugged the church wall, moving as hurriedly as I could in this awkward crab like motion, until I reached the base of the ladder. Once in position I paused to review my tactics. The simplest solution is often the best, and I set to work.

I opened my coat and uncoiled the rope wound around my waist. It had accompanied me on all my nightly excursions. Luckily it was neither very long, nor very heavy. I slipped around the front of the ladder, which the thieves had thoughtfully positioned in the shadows, and fastened one end of the rope around the bottom rung. After testing its security, I stepped back several paces and, holding the other end, I pulled as hard as I could.

I surprised myself by my own strength, or perhaps it was the frosty ground which aided my success. Either way the bottom of the ladder slid towards me so rapidly that I found myself running backwards to avoid its collapse. It toppled almost silently, except when it hit the gravel. In any other circumstances this would have gone unnoticed, but in that stillness you could hear the proverbial pin drop. Much less an aluminium ladder on stone.

My "friends" must have been some distance away, or just had slower reflexes. Whatever the cause, by the time they arrived at the roof edge, I had untied the rope and took up my post against the church wall.

I didn't understand a word of the forthcoming commotion, nor did I need to. I could easily interpret its content. It was the classic case of "when thieves fall out". Obviously they were blaming each other for their predicament.

I have a strong theory that a lot of physical violence nowadays is due to the frustration of being unable to vocalise anger. It seemed appropriate outside this congregational chapel to remember a line from the film Cromwell: "when men run out of words they reach for their swords".

Well the quarrelling pair had no weapons as such, but fists always provide a convenient substitute. From the racket above it seemed that the time had passed for obscenities – in any language.

I clearly heard the thud of bone connecting with bone. All caution appeared thrown to the wind – a few seconds later so was something else. I heard a cry just before a large shape fell past me and landed just feet in front of my hiding place.

Horrified, even in this restricted light, I saw the object was a body. For the first time in my career I felt a sense of guilt. Yes, they were callous and greedy, but neither of these vices deserved a death penalty. What had I done?

Gratefully my question was answered immediately, when the inert figure suddenly burst back to life. From the outline the casualty was the smaller individual, but what he lacked in size he more than made up for in lung capacity. He began screaming his head off like the proverbial stuck pig.It is a strong belief that the noisier the invalid the less severe the injury. In which case I was relieved to hear that no serious harm had been done. But I had another dilemma: I could not let this go without summoning help. The injured man had got over the shock and recovered his wind sufficiently to sit up. However he could not appear to stand up and when I saw the unnatural angle of his right leg I could understand why. This made the matter more urgent. He required immediate help, or otherwise risk amputation, and I would not have that on my conscience.

I need not have worried: the uproar was already drawing unwelcome attention. Ironically this was good news for the thieves, but bad for myself. As fortune would have it a passing policeman was the first witness to the mayhem.

It was time for my departure. Since all attention was on the wounded culprit and his stranded companion, it was easy to make my escape.

My journey home followed the scenic route, with enough cover to avoid detection. Just as well, since at one point an ambulance raced past: no doubt carrying paramedics. A few yards farther and more blue lights sent me into someone's hedge. This time police back up, no doubt carrying handcuffs. I didn't see the fire brigade to complete the set. I imagine there was no need. The police would utilise the ladder thoughtfully provided.

It took some time to arrive home via this circuitous means, and when I got there I did some serious soul searching. Yes, they were heartless criminals, but I had never considered such dramatic results. I had envisaged a lesson learnt without physical injury. What if he had serious internal injuries, or lost his leg?

I could rationalise events as well as I could: if they had not fought he would not have fallen. Indeed if they had not been on the roof stealing in the first place. What ifs were all very well, but there was that irritating conscience again. Maybe I was in the wrong job.

I had removed the ladder, therefore I had more than a little responsibility for the outcome, more than a little cause for reproach. That guilt cost me a few more sleepless nights, even though I discontinued my nocturnal wanderings.

This insomnia continued until the news eventually

made the local newspaper. I breathed a long sigh of relief. The headline set the tone for the article: "Bungling Burglars." The fact that one suffered a fractured leg was pushed to the back of the story. The predominant theme was black comedy, tinged with a sense of poetic justice. Much was made of the felons eastern European roots – which led to another editorial on immigration.

It took more in depth reading to find the detail which interested me. The injury was isolated and uncomplicated, just requiring a plaster cast. So much so that the patient had already been discharged and rejoined his partner in police custody.

I was satisfied that no long term harm had been done, except possibly to the miscreants' dignity. If that deterred them from future lead stripping expeditions then my mission accomplished.

On the whole we had all escaped with very little trouble. The real losers in this adventure was probably the poor old overstretched NHS service, who had to deal with the fallout – no pun intended. For that I still feel a little guilty.

Aside from that, there were a lot more smiles at the local church, who felt their faith in some divine power had been restored. Everyone, including the press and police, saw the incident as an "act of God". No one for a second guessed that deliverance came from a much less exalted source.

Chapter Nine

THE PLAYER'S TALE

The next weeks passed quietly. The cold weather had set in and even the novelty of snow soon vanished. The landscape turned from a picture perfect winter wonderland to a dangerous combination, with the qualities of a compacted ice rink, and dirty hazardous slush trap. Anything when taken to excess out stays its welcome and becomes a source of complaint. Weather is no exception, certainly not in the U.K., where it fills the gap in any dialogue to the point it dominates the entireconversation.

Moods, like viruses, are frequently contagious and I caught this one. Possibly because I was susceptible and weakened through lack of sleep. Whatever the cause my body reacted as it would to any other invader. In times of stress, mental or physical, nature takes over from reason and tells the body what it needs. If we are wise we listen, and in this instance I needed rest.

After a few days of recuperation I felt ready to face the world and my thoughts once more. With my mind revived, it gave me the chance for a rational post mortem of my conduct.

With hindsight I cannot say I regretted my actions, but the near tragic outcome did make me consider the wisdom of my intervention.

I have never deluded myself that I was on a kind of noble quest: some sort of innocent instrument of divine judgement. Indeed, as I have said, I am not even sure I actually believe an higher power, let alone its justice. But there had been a clear intention to punish according to the severity of the offence, and in this instance my "mission" had almost caused catastrophic results. Perhaps I should quit while I was ahead.

Unfortunately, for my good intentions, evil does not take a break. Every day it tempts us through pride, greed, envy, anger, lust, gluttony, sloth – otherwise known as the seven deadly sins. My only surprise is that there are just seven. Despite their small number they are certainly extensive. They can be seen everyday, in any place, in any group of humanity: regardless of religion, or lack of it. In, thankfully, rarer instances, all of them encased in one loathsome specimen.

So far most of my work has stemmed from an unhealthy obsession with the second Sin. Greed is undeniably the catalyst for most crime – urged on by envy. Greed is typically associated with money, but it is not confined to the filthy lucre. Power and fame are also cravings for the avaricious: Sadly, in our modern materialist state sin has become a virtue. What were flaws in human nature have now become assets. The individual who grabs more than their share, at the expense of the less fortunate, or more ethical, is rewarded and honoured.

No surprise then that greed, in one form or another, had

been the main impetus for my exploits. All this was about to change. While I cannot deny that power plays its part in the next scenario, it is a sin lower down the conventional biblical order which predominates.

Lust may be relegated to fourth place, but from this all manner of terrible suffering may follow. Desire, without love or compassion, may begin almost "harmlessly" with consensual seduction. But lust can deteriorate rapidly into a downward spiral of self satisfaction leading to rape and murder. This story begins at the bestial bottom of the slippery slope.

Any justification which contains excuses for adult sexual abuse of children is an argument I don't care to consider. Even more so when that exploitation is so calculated and well planned. As far as I was concerned there was no defence: the verdict was a forgone conclusion; sentence was passed and execution pending.

But the circumstances of this case really begin with a little known fact about me. I enjoy gaming.

Gaming, as in video game. I have never seen the satisfaction of donating my hard earned finances to the already overflowing coffers of the online/offline gambling industry. Besides my boredom threshold is such that more than half an hour pressing buttons, or pulling levers, on a ravenous fruit machine drives me to distraction. For me its like working on a production line. In a factory where, instead of receiving wages in compensation for the monotony, you pay money for the privilege. It has simply never made practical sense to me, let alone financial logic.

With this outlook it is hardly surprising that I prefer the more cerebral games: involving role play and problem solving. But we all have our Achilles heel and mine is the satisfaction of collection. I love obtaining achievements or trophies, depending on the game console. If you are a fellow gamer this needs no clarification, if you are not: believe me its not worth the explanation.

Despite natural preferences my gaming name and avatar have been known to show up on the multiplayer lists for several 'shoot em up' games. In fact I'll admit, with embarrassment, that I became so hooked on one that I wasted far too many hours and weeks in obtaining full prestige. My 'reward' was a virtual reality Golden gun, which I activated before realising it made me not only the most wanted target, but also the most visible. If you have your own avatar, explanation is unnecessary: if not, be grateful. Suffice it to say the first deadly sin will not tempt me again – in this respect at least.

One great attraction of online gaming is some sense of comradeship. If you feel lonely you boot up your system and immediately have the world in your living room.

Another huge advantage is the gratifying knowledge that my online "friends" have no idea who, or what, I am. I never use a mike, so any connection is controlled via messaging. While words can sometimes be ambiguous and a cause of misunderstanding; they are also satisfyingly liberating. Texts provide the means to enjoy the archetypal best of both worlds: companionship without commitment. In this way the borders of my personal space are defined, protected and self regulated. If you have not guessed by now, control is a major defect in my character. Perhaps that should be the eighth sin.

However like most innovations with the potential for

good, they also contain the seeds for their own perversion. What for me, and probably the majority of gamers, provides harmless privacy and security; for others presents an opportunity for camouflage and disturbing manipulation.

In my own case, for example, few of my opponents would imagine they are playing with a sixty plus woman. And of that knowledge I think the most shocking disclosure would be my gender.

Technology seems to be viewed as a masculine pursuit. Certainly in the gaming world you enter the domain of barefaced male prejudice. No one seems to believe that females are either interested or capable. This is borne out by some of the explicit sexist avatars available, and the preponderance of testosterone fuelled games. Even those featuring a heroine are sure to depict her with lavish proportions and meagre coverage.

Sadly this biased view seems to begin with boys and continue to men. Although I would be hard pressed to decide which is the chicken and egg in this cycle, since most youngsters adopt learned attitudes and behaviour. And let's not forget the influence of our old friends: media and society.

Whatever comes first, there seems to be a general consensus of opinion that competitive success is not only unnatural, but even impossible, for those of the X chromosome persuasion.

In the real world this is manifest in sport, where females, if indeed they are allowed to participate, are frequently undervalued. Yet ironically it is in the women's events where a sense of sportsMANship survives. For most of their male counterparts, sport has been tainted by our old friend, greed:

allowing personal ambition and money to dominate. The emphasis has changed from a fair play philosophy to one of win at any cost. There is no longer any consolation for the loser in the ancient noble adage " it matters not whether you win or lose, but how you play the game".

But I digress: so step off the feminist soapbox and back to the subject: the benefits and pitfalls of internet anonymity.

The advantages I have already mentioned, as long as you don't fall into your own trap. Never be naïve enough to take appearances at face value. Always be prepared to consider that your adversary may be someone you would avoid in broad daylight, let alone a dark alley. Remember too that said individual may not be sitting safely a thousand miles away, but perhaps living right around the corner! But most important of all, never forget that they may be liars.

Parents and children disregard these warnings at their peril. All too often media horror stories testify to the dangers of such negligence. It makes no more sense for a child to be unsupervised on the web, as it would for her/him to be left alone with a complete stranger in the park. Yet children sit in the privacy of their rooms, talking to who knows who, about who knows what, for hours on end.

Despite the best efforts of internet security and governments the WWW is a very real, and deadly trap for the young. It is the refuge for the most depraved and spineless paedophiles, who weave their own web of lies and squat in it.

It is a common belief that children are more street wise nowadays, but the old saying holds true "you cannot put an old head on young shoulders". Children are perhaps as trusting and innocent as they ever were. Except in this technological era, the world is open to them and they to all its dangers.

Of course predators understand this, and use it to full advantage. You cannot blame the children, although their abusers usually try to. This is hardly surprising: even adults routinely accept gossip and rumour as fact. You only have to see how many readers treat tabloid journalism as truth to prove this. It is left for the more cynical of us imagine to that a game name of princess2000 could in reality disguise a sick pervert getting off on chatting up children. If only it were to stop there.

Having no young children in my family this potential threat had not been a cause for personal concern. This situation was all about to change.

One of the few people privileged to know about my secret online activity was the granddaughter of an old friend. Emma was an only child and the apple of her doting parents' eyes. If she was spoilt then her character gave no negative sign; she was a perfect caring, imaginative and outgoing ten year old.

Last Christmas I had bought the girl her greatest wish: a games console. Her parents, while considerably younger than myself, had somehow managed to remain blissfully ignorant of such entertainment. So it was left for me to set up the system. The location, for mutual convenience, was designated as Emma's bedroom. No warning bells yet. But I followed manufacturer's advice and put in place certain recommended security precautions.

We selected a suitably innocuous gaming name for her: nothing either too feminine or macho. Likewise we chose a nondescript avatar: a cartoon character I recall. My last act was to send a friend request to myself, so that we could correspond, share games, and I could act as guardian, if need be..

A year had passed and there had been no occasion for interference. In fact everything had gone well until the last month. Online chats, and invitations to join her games, had become less frequent until they were non existent. A quick scan of her activity log seemed to show an attraction for one particular game. This fascination was no cause for concern: it was not a restricted 18+ category, but a children's role play.

So, unwisely, as it turned out, I put her behaviour down to awakening hormones. I thought, with a little disappointment, that perhaps I was no longer cool. It is amazing how quickly older people can morph from being a source of pride to a total embarrassment.

If I am honest though, I was a bit preoccupied in the new year: trying to maim a roof stripper!

It wasn't until a routine telephone call to my friend, her grandmother, that I felt the first symptoms of anxiety. It seemed that the child's detachment was not restricted to her internet persona. She had become physically withdrawn, mainly to her bedroom. The conversation ended with the promise that I would arrange a visit with the worried parents to try to talk to Emma.

In my experience children, and indeed adults, will more likely confide in friends than family. I am not a psychologist, so would not attempt an analysis of this behaviour, but it is a fact.

I had already had a nagging suspicion that the games console was at the centre of this problem. She seldom spent any time with her parents or friends. The only contact she had with the outside world, out of school hours, was through her bedroom. This was unhealthy, and if she was ill then it was my responsibility. As soon as I severed the link to my friend, I dialled her daughter.

Although I was careful not transfer my own fears, I realised that the situation had deteriorated so much that I agreed to call later that evening.

My welcome was as warm as ever: the parents either had made no link between my gift or did not apportion any blame. Maybe they were simply desperate for help.

It was just after teatime, but Emma had already retired for the evening. As I started up the stairs I glanced back: it was painful to see the hope in their faces. I stood outside the girl's door for a moment and took a deep breath. I knocked and waited: you don't begin this sort of intrusion by an act of disrespect. I was just going to risk another knock when a small voice asked "who is it?" I had always held the honorary title of aunt and used it now to reply.

She was either too polite to refuse, or was genuinely pleased to see me. It was hard to tell from her apathetic manner. It didn't matter to me, whatever the reason I was inside her room – the inner sanctum. There was an abnormal awkwardness: we always had an open and lively relationship. But such was our history that a few candid remarks broke the spell and tension. We were soon sitting together catching up on ourmutual interests – which of course included gaming.

It didn't take long for Emma to get to the heart of the matter. She was not by nature a recluse. I have never known her sulk once in her short life. Another trait we have in common: we both consider sulking a complete waste of time – our time.

Over the bag of favourite sweets I had brought as a peace offering we shared our recent internet experiences. Mine consisted of humorous anecdotes about the antics of fellow gamers: who can always be relied upon to provide laughter capable to rendering you helpless. Once we had recovered from a refreshing 'fit of the giggles' Emma began her own contribution.

The beginning was harmless enough. She had bought a new game on the recommendation of several school friends – it was this which had occupied her time over the past month.

The offline story had recorded an album of self photographs posted onto her profile for the benefit of friends only. The online section of this game had brought the usual crop of new friend requests. She accepted these and had commenced the usual round of text messaging. This is quite common and usually centres around the game: offering support and advice.

When those texts start to focus on personal issues that sets my BS radar working. Apparently there had been one such inquisitive individual who recently joined her list. I had continually warned Emma not to answer any request for private details of her life. As I waited her response to my question I mentally crossed all fingers – and toes – that she had listened. It turned out she had. Not only that, but she had kept copies of all the received messages.

It was a long record going back a couple of months. The texts began with brief messages about the game, but within a week progressed to add subtle hints about Emma's home. When these were ignored more information followed about the other's life, including the "fact" that "Debbie" was a 9 year old living in the mid West of the U.S.A. There was a lot of writing but very little real detail. Emma, bless her heart, had given nothing away under this continuous barrage.

The final message from Debbie first arrived a week ago, but had been resent with monotonous regularity every day since. I had arrived in the nick of time. Emma had held up well under the bombardment, but was reaching breaking point. No wonder she was distracted and withdrawn.

I read the text and its content made an whole belfry of alarm bells clang.

Debbie was shortly visiting England with her parents and wanted to meet her new keyboard pal. But it was the postscript which troubled me. The suggestion that they meet up in secret, without either set of parents' knowledge.

As I thought about all the implications and resolutions, I looked around the room for inspiration. My eyes automatically paused on the silent gamesconsole: the object of all this misery. In doing so I glimpsed a small device sitting on top of the monitor/tv, and suddenly my brain received a flash of clarity.

Emma had done all the right things but she had been betrayed – by the spy in her bedroom. A tiny web cam which, I now recalled, had downloaded the image of its owner for all her friends to view.

Debbie was a friend, yet why had she never referred to the fact that she had seen these pictures. That was odd. Most young girls would have passed some comment. It gave me cause to look again, more carefully, at those photographs.

I saw a series of portraits in various poses: mugging for the camera, but looking closer, I saw something else. The wall behind Emma held a sort of notice board: in pride of place was a poster for a school play. I remembered that I had been to see this last autumn: my "niece" had had a leading role.

I turned around and studied the advertisement: among the details were the school name and other useful information – like directions!! How easy would it be to read this: simple with a photo software package and good magnifying glass.

It took me a faction of a second to reach a decision.

First things first. I suggested that this "friend" should be deleted from the console. In fact I supervised this removal and, I am afraid, put enough fear of God into Emma to ensure that she would never reopen the relationship. I felt briefly sorry for the young American girl if this was a genuine approach, but all my instincts told me that it was not.

Secondly, the offending photographs were despatched into the ether. Of course I know that such deletions are never really lost and technophiles can recover discarded information. But this was just the first phase of an operation, which would not end until I was convinced of Emma's safety.

Finally, I removed the web cam and offending game. Emma came downstairs with me and I left the family reunited after a brief explanation. This included edited details of Emma's persecution, but excluded the photographic blunder and any hint that the situation was not resolved. I saw no point in alarming them further. If things went as planned "Debbie" would have other matters to occupy her time in the next few weeks.

Satisfied I went home. Time was important: I went

straight to my own console and turned it on. I inserted the borrowed game and watched as the machine greedily sucked it in.

Once installed and loaded I selected the multiplayer option and awaited connection. It was late evening in the UK and, if previous habits were observed, my subject should be arriving home from her American elementary school.

I spent the next couple of hours surfing through the game: dropping in and out of various teams. I acquired my own share of "friends" and accepted: it might look odd if I selected just one and declined all others.

Still no sign of Debbie. The infinite variety of game names, which are usually amusing or intriguing, were becoming tedious. I was about ready to pack it all in when I saw a notification flash up on the screen: an alias I knew as well as my own was joining the game.

I didn't stay long, just enough to send a couple of my own "friend requests" : one for appearances sake: the other a cast line with hook. Before I logged out, and shut down the machine for the night, I noticed one other thing. The signal strength for my new friend was high: perhaps too strong to cover all those miles of land and ocean.

A response awaited me the next morning.

In the meantime I had been busy. I downloaded an image from one of my old picture agency sites onto my games server. It showed a young girl, around 10 years old smiling at the camera. It had taken a while to select, but not too long – picture research, after all, had been my business. The main requirement was that the child looked natural – no chocolate box advertising perfection required here.

Another half an hour later and my alter ego had a new

background. My child self now sat in a "pink princess" bedroom, courtesy of my own professional photo studio software. I checked it carefully and then added my 'piece de resistance.' In view on the desk in front of 'me' was a London Transport Oyster card.

Before transferring this image to the games console I went through the system with a fine tooth comb. I had no idea how proficient my adversary was at computer technology. My best strategy would be to hope the best while preparing for the worst. There must be nothing to tie me with any other links which could reveal my real identity.

But there was a major weak spot: my trophy/achievements list which was online and a permanent memorial to my vanity. Would he read it – yes, of course he would! But could I explain it – yes, of course I could. I had created a fictitious little girl, newly christened Samantha. I could easily provide her with an older brother: fortuitously now away at college. A parting gift had been his games console.

My final act had been to delete all previous friends. This obviously, and most essentially, included Emma. There must be no connection between us: for our mutual protection.

Then I downloaded "my" image: the hook was now baited.

A bite came that evening. So began a concentrated offensive. It was difficult at times to judge whom was the more successful "groomer". This process could not be rushed, but, at the same time, I had to keep up the dialogue to give no time for reprisals against Emma. Nevertheless this recent rejection could be useful: it would make my antagonist more frustrated and less cautious. As long as I remembered that it could also make him dangerous.

The more I learnt about "Debbie" the stronger my

conviction of gender and age. This was a male, and one much older than the school child pretence. I hoped that my feminine instinct was accurate. Apart from this intuition, I had one big advantage in this game of cat and mouse: at least half my representation was fact.

As suspicions of my opponent's motives were increasingly confirmed I moved away from this objective and towards another. I now had a fair idea of his agenda: I just needed to help him along to its conclusion. As it turned out I had absolutely no idea what I was dealing with.

This charade continued for a month, until one evening I checked my message box. It was a case of history repeating itself: with a disappointing lack of innovation.

Surprise, surprise, Debbie's family were once again planning a visit and, guess what, an invitation was extended to meet up. I could not believe how quickly and effortlessly events were proceeding. Time now to reel in my catch: little did I imagine what a shark was at the end.

Now came the same disturbing condition. This must be a clandestine meeting: Debbie's parents did not approve of their daughter's cyber liaisons.

I restrained myself from asking too many questions: I was playing the role of a gullible young girl excited by the prospect of adventure. In reality I was well prepared for this contingency. There had been enough time to plan a suitable venue, and by now every criteria was fulfilled.

For my guest, it must be somewhere which raised no doubts, or red flags. Somewhere in the London suburbs would seem a logical suggestion given the photographic evidence I planted. For my own benefit the main consideration was parking access.

A time and date was agreed for a week hence. We were probably both feverishly working at concocting cover stories. I just hoped that I was the only one who knew this.

For my part I gave, what I considered, a plausible explanation that I lived nearby and could slip away for an hour to the local high street. I had already recced the area and selected a convenient burger bar, with plenty of on street parking.

I was fascinated to read the response: it was a masterpiece of invention. My young friend found no fault with the plan. She claimed that her elder sister could be persuaded to accompany her on this excursion from their West End hotel.

The day arrived, and I left home early to take the motorway to my North London destination. I stopped once en route to fill up my tank: I had no idea where this journey would take me. Even with this detour I was in position a good half an hour before 11am, the appointed hour.

I parked in a space near the café, where I had a perfect view of the designated rendezvous. I confirmed parking regulations: as expectedI had a couple of hours leeway. Then I locked and left the vehicle to join the café patrons. It was busy, so I shared a table with a fellow diner. Two retired ladies sharing tea and sandwiches on a beautiful spring day. A perfect camouflage since it was unhappily based on partial truth. I had taken the precaution of emphasising my decrepitude by the application of an appalling blue rinse. I had also dug out an old walking stick from the attic.

Well I had my cover: how would my friend appear? Probably not as a young American girl, but if she did, then I could finish my lunch and go home. But I did not think it likely, any more than I thought to see the stereotypical dirty old man. There would be no black plastic mac. As we have learnt to our children's cost, paedophiles come in all shapes and disguises.

The time came and went, but no one appeared. Ten minutes later a car slowed down and reversed into a space opposite the café. The sole occupant, its driver, thoughtfully wound the window down. From what I could see he was in his late fifties and the exact opposite of the proverbial flasher. Smartly dressed and groomed (no pun intended), he could have passed for a business man meeting a colleague, or an impatient husband awaiting his wife.

What was it then that made me doubt either possibility? Perhaps he was just too perfect. One thing I had learnt: when anything looks too good to be true, it usually is.

My lunch companion was requesting her bill, and I did likewise. We wished each goodbye at the door, like a pair of old friends, and went our separate ways. Mine consisted of an exaggerated hobble towards my vehicle. I made a meal of getting in: delaying tactics while keeping a sneaky eye on the street ahead.

There was no one suspicious hanging around the café: except the aforesaid driver, who still remained in his vehicle. He was obviously becoming restless, because the fingers of his right hand drummed a furious rhythm on the roof. To fill my own time I bent over and took a notebook from the dashboard. A record of the registration would do no harm and may prove useful.

In doing so I had cause to amend my initial impression. This was neither a business, nor rental car. There was a sticker in the rear window warning "child on board" and the outline of a teddy bear shaped sun screen. If this proved to be my man I was not shocked, or even surprised. Most deviants hide in plain sight under the cloak of conformity. Family life is one of the cornerstones of social respectability.

It was while I was staring at the child friendly emblem that I noticed the right indicator blink in preparation to pull out. Fortunately we were both pointing in the same direction, so it was easy to follow. But I had to be careful, so I forced myself to wait until another car slotted between us.

We had come so far but the next miles would be the most critical. So I kept at least one, sometimes two, cars behind my objective. This game of mobile hide and seek continued through the landscaped suburbs into the real countryside. As more and more cars turned off to alternative destinations I was forced to drop back to avoid detection. Eventually aid came in the form of an impatient driver, who annoyed by my tentative manoeuvring, overtook and provided a new shield. I could almost hear his views on women drivers!

So we continued in this convoy, and soon doubts began to creep in. What if I was wrong? What if this is a perfectly innocent husband returning home to his family? What if that family is in Scotland? How far do I go?

We didn't travel very much further before my questions were answered. The brake lights of the car in front of me shot on and I clearly saw the teddy bear motif as it made a sharp right turn. The motorist, already aggravated by my driving, gave an angry blast and crude finger gesture after the offending vehicle. As I had been maintaining a safe distance, we avoided collision. But the incident brought me an unexpected bonus. As we came to a virtual halt it gave me the chance to risk a quick sideways glance. I saw the "child on board" sticker bouncing away down a narrow private lane.

Now I was faced with a decision: although I really had no choice. Having literally travelled so far I could not just carry on. I must find somewhere to stop and regroup my thoughts. A convenient lay by appeared as if in answer to my problem. I pulled in and reviewed my next move. A bend sheltered my vehicle from the lane entrance, but it also obscured my view. I could not use this as an observation spot. So I did the only thing I could, I locked the car and retraced my route on foot. My one thought as I made my way along the grass verge was "what if he pulled out and I was caught in this compromising position?" If he was wary and felt threatened this was a perfect place – for him, not me. There was little traffic and plenty of undergrowth.

This sobering thought accelerated my steps and I soon reached the dirt road which led to who knew what. While this thought was hardly enticing, it was even less palatable to stand around exposed on a deserted country road. So I stepped into the welcoming shelter of the budding trees, made myself comfortable, and waited.

Almost 30 minutes later I heard an engine and blended further into my camouflage. The car emerged from a turn at the end of the track and drove slowly towards my hiding place. Instinctively I ducked down and held my breath. But it continued on to the junction with the main road and concern now switched to my abandoned car. What if it aroused his suspicions? I hardly had time to begin planning a strategy when I saw the vehicle skid out from the gravel: turning left and back the way we had come.

I forced myself to wait another 15 minutes – choosing

to err on the side of caution. Then I followed the tree line along the drive towards the blind bend. My decision was two fold: firstly I did not want to leave any sort of track in the soft dirt; secondly, as yet I had no way of knowing if he had an accomplice.

With this thought in mind I crept deeper into cover as I rounded the corner. What I saw did nothing to reduce my vigilance. In front of me a clearing had opened up, and within it sat an object I recognised: a large static caravan.

Most caravans have a similar layout and I immediately recognised the lounge and bedroom areas, even with all the windows boarded up. Despite a basic resemblance to my own holiday home it was a couple of decades older. Built in an age before their manufacturers attempted to mimic house design: complete with patios and imitation roof tiles. No, the mobile home in front of me made no pretence of bricks and mortar, it was unashamedly proud of its aluminium construction.

In this instance familiarity bred confidence rather than contempt. It took only a few more moments for me to access the situation and relax. Call it some sort of sixth sense, or just logic. If I could not see in then no one was looking out. There was no sign of transportation, and for anyone living in this remote hovel that would be a necessity.

It was obviously deserted, but I hugged my old friends the bushes and circled the derelict old mobile home. The area around the property provided no cover: the earth was barren with paving slabs. As I edged closer the blank windows looked more ominous: were they keeping intruders out, or keeping someone/thing in?

The caravan had none of usual amenities: no generator,

water or gas tanks littered the yard. This neglect, added to its dilapidated and isolated condition, made this a perfect bolt hole. No one, even a vagrant with a less rigid interpretation of the concept, would call this a home.

The very last thing I felt like doing at this moment was the very thing I had to. I had to see inside this uninviting place, or abandon the whole scheme. That was unthinkable – too many innocent lives were at stake. One in particular, Emma, and the thought that she could have ended up here: but behind those thin cold metal walls.

Forcing that thought aside I found, what I knew to be the window to the "master" bedroom. Of course it was too high, but a nearby log solved that problem. From this position, and the help of my dependable multi tool, it was relatively easy to unscrew the board and prise open the concealed window. No wonder the windows had been secured: I found, nearly at the cost of my fingers, that the glass was broken into shards. With the greatest care, and an extra pair of gloves, I climbed in.

The thought of accidental discovery did not concern me: only the fact that the owner may yet return. This had obviously been his hideaway for some time: it had been well selected and secured. His protection was therefore now my protection.

I turned on my torch and panned around: what I saw it resembled a man made cave. But as I looked I saw it was something more. Something no animal, however savage, would have inflicted on their young. This was not a place of safety, but misery. Against one wall was a bed, if you could call such a foul contraption by such an everyday term. There was nothing extraordinary about this article except its condition. It was unmade because there was nothing to make: just a bare worn mattress. I didn't even want to contemplate a child being brought in here, but there was worst to come. At first I thought the mattress was an unusually deep shade, but then my torch revealed more detail. The colour was in fact the result of extensive dark staining.

I had had enough and spun around to find the door, which I knew must be behind me. In doing I almost collided with an object to my right. It rocked a little, but seemed to have stabilised by the time I got the flashlight steadied. This was indeed a chamber of horrors, but complete with every modern convenience – including a video camera and tripod.

By this time I just wanted to get out of this monument to man's depravity, but now it was even more impossible to walk away. I knew then that what I saw I would take to my grave: because I could share this knowledge with no one. The only way I could live with this evil was to end it.

So, God knows how, but I forced myself to remain long enough to finalise a plan and then left the same way I came. I meticulously secured the board as best I could, and returned the log to its original indentation. I stood back, surveyed my handiwork, and took a deep breath of fresh air.

As I walked back to my car my hand rested on my jacket pocket, and the one item I had removed from that hell hole. I had considered long and hard before I took it, but it was an essential part of my scheme. It had been in the bedroom, and given the fact that my target had returned empty handed, I didn't think he would miss it.

I was grateful for the increased rush hour traffic on my way home: it kept my body busy and my mind from other thoughts.

Back home a message was already waiting. It took several minutes and a great deal of self control to raise the courage to respond. I now knew what was at the other end of that connection and where this text had been sent from. The games console I had found in the caravan living room, powered by a small petrol generator and serviced courtesy of a local wi fi hot spot.

Initially I had wondered why so much expensive technology had been left in such a vulnerable location, but the answer was simple: security. It would be far more precarious to carry around such evidence in the car, and risk discovery by inquisitive police or children. Oh yes somewhere there were children who called this creature "father" – of that I was certain.

The acquisition of all this knowledge made it even more vital that I deal with this cold-blooded pervert. I had to keep him on the hook: I could not let him get away. To that end I had to arrange another meeting. So I wrote back, making the apology that I couldn't get away from mum. Holding my breath, and offering up a rare prayer, I suggested that we try again tomorrow afternoon. My mother had a dental appointment and I had the excuse of a friend's birthday party. Gritting my teeth I added that if this were impossible, "not to worry we could meet up on some other trip".

Would he take the lure, or had I scared him off? There is an old saying which is crude but true " a stiff dick has no conscience" and I hoped in this case, no commonsense either. I was depending on that now. How and when would he respond? He must live close to the caravan to access the console – that thought made my blood run cold: how close had I come to a confrontation. I need not have worried: a reply did not arrive until early the next morning. He no doubt had a day job in the area which provided cover to visit his hideaway.

Yes, "Debbie" had been a bit put out, but was still keen to meet her friend. The imaginary sister was coerced into another chaperone job for her non existent sibling . I replied with, what I considered, an understandable question "where have you been and would you like to make it later in the week" My correspondent was eager to the point of reckless. No today it would be and whinged about unreasonable parental control preventing her contacting me earlier.

We arranged to meet same place, different time: at 1pm to be precise. We broke the connection and a few seconds later a notification flashed up on my screen. My friend had signed off.

I looked at the clock: it was still only a few minutes to nine. An early departure was out of the question: the shorter my presence around the caravan the better. I had left the console on: set to register any online activity from "Debbie." All was silent. I had barely eaten since yesterday's lunch at the cafÈ and that combined with the tension made me feel nauseous. So I filled the time and my empty stomach with a hearty breakfast. I am not sure I actually tasted anything, and the outcome was a spectacular bout of heartburn. Liberal doses of antacids eventually eased the pain, just in time for me to start my journey.

It was a good 90 minute drive to the first village I had discovered on my route back yesterday. I estimated it would take another 30 minutes to park and walk back to the secluded caravan. Once there a further 30 minutes to break in and prepare. I checked the offline status one final time, turned off the system and left.

The road trip took a little less time than anticipated, the walk a little more. I found the caravan as forsaken as ever, with no sign of life. Now came the tricky bit. I could not risk using the log and possible detection. Luckily I had foreseen and planned for this situation. The backpack had been an inspired accessory: who looks twice at a hiker on a country road?

But it has also proved an invaluable practical asset. I now put it down beneath the bedroom window and took out my solution: a fold up step. It wasn't very high, but it was enough to reach the window. I threw the backpack into the room ahead me before climbing up after it. But a blue plastic step was, if anything, more distinctive than a log. It had one plus however: with the attachment of a small length of rope I could haul it up after me.

With everything reunited I folded the step and replaced it in the backpack. At the same time I removed the torch, and a plastic carrier bag, before I secured the window and plunged myself into darkness. I nudged the pack under the bed with my foot. I would either recover it later, or have no further need of it – or anything else come to that. I was under no illusion that I was dealing with an extremely dangerous individual. We had come a long way from the image of a solitary paedophile. To say that I stood in the lair of fiend sounds dramatic, but was an understatement of the truth. What adequate description was there for such a thing masquerading as a human being. A creature not merely content to inflict suffering for personal pleasure, but to share that with a foul network of like minded sadists. This was not pure supposition: proof sat on a table in the living room.

The evidence remained where I left it yesterday. In pride

of place was the incriminating games console, whose data would eventually lead back to me. This had been my Holy Grail. Whatever else happened today, if I survived this must not. Not yet though, it still had an important role to play.

To one side of this sat an innocent enough looking laptop. Except I knew what it contained. Media downloaded from the camera set up in the bedroom. One glimpse had been enough to confirm what I suspected about the genre of this particular photographic hobby. Suffice it to say the contents would not have passed any official classification.

Enlightenment had made my decisions easier. This man, for want of a better word, had made his choice years ago. He could have selected self control, instead of self gratification. Now it was my turn. I could ring the authorities and have him put out of harm's way for a few years, or at best a lifetime. Neither was enough for me, I would take my own punishment, if it came, without blaming my victims or some psychological disorder. It took me a heartbeat to reach a verdict and take up position.

I felt strangely relaxed, even though what was in fact minutes felt like hours. Through the thin metal walls I could faintly hear passing traffic on the road. Then a different sound: an engine idling followed by the distinctive crunch of tyres on gravel. Somewhere outside I heard a car stop and the engine die.

I flexed my limbs in the cramped recess: it would be disastrous to seize up now. Footsteps approached and the closer they came the faster my pulse rate. Thank goodness for a recent health check, otherwise I may have feared a stroke or heart attack.

As it was I just had to contend with a psychopath – who

was just turning a key in the lock. There was a brief flash of daylight as he entered, but it lasted a moment and I had chosen my concealment well. A second rejection had evidently not improved "Debbie's" temper, since there was a lot of unladylike language. This angry monologue continued all through the start up of the generator, and boot up of the games system.

From my retreat I heard some very uncomplimentary remarks and threats about my gender, in which the term "bitches" featured prominently. Then, in the subdued light from the monitor, I saw a large pair of suit clad legs invade my space. Of course I was prepared for this: I was after all under the table which held his paraphernalia.

It is well known fact that no male can follow the advice usually offered to women. They cannot keep their legs together. Whether this is a physical impossibility, or a form of conceit I do not know, but it served my purpose. As I crouched there, I felt like a weird gynaecologist. For all those insensitive male invasions of my intimate regions I was about to take full revenge. In my right hand I held the taser I had removed from his "torture chamber"the day before. I could hardly miss at this range, and scored a direct hit in the testicles. He jolted back, overturning the chair, and I jumped out ready to deliver a second jolt if necessary. It was not. He was jerking flat on the floor, not even capable of clutching his injured member.

Choice was still possible, but as I looked at that twitching body I only saw his victims. No, I had made my decision and there was no going back. Anger suppressed any pity, but there was another emotion I had never felt before – pleasurable anticipation. What had I become: at that moment

I didn't care. Whatever it was this twisted man had created it, and now he would reap the consequences.

Remorse could come later. Cold blooded rage was the impetus which had me reaching inside my jacket to extract the plastic bag and the tape it contained. Fury was what he saw as I bent over him and whispered "how does it feel – hurts doesn't it." But the last thing he saw was satisfaction as I promised "never mind it will soon be over." I stuffed the plastic bag over his head and taped it shut. I don't know how aware he was in his last moments of the irony, but I hope so.

I stood back and watched him die. Horrible though it was, his death was probably the most peaceful and merciful these walls had witnessed.

After he became still I collected my backpack from the bedroom. I gathered up the console and any accessories, including games. All of them I noticed aimed at the younger end of the market and specifically girls. It was essential that the police have no clue to the game connection, as this link could be followed directly back to me.

The laptop I left. There was a possibility that my game name may be stored within, but it also provided a valuable lead to the paedophile ring. It was worth the risk to close them down, and, hopefully, shut them up for a very long time. While protecting the future, it would also bring resolution to the past. The photographic data it contained may help trace any missing children, or their bodies. The crime scene which surrounded me was that ghastly.

I could never describe what I witnessed there: no satisfactory words exist. Suffice it to say that my estimation on the depths of human depravity sank to an all time low. I am not sure that it every really recovered.

I shouldered the backpack and took a final look around the room. Just to check nothing had been overlooked. Satisfied I left by the front door for the first and last time.

When I removed the console from the table I found the caravan key where its owner had dropped it. It was attached to a ring with a novelty minuscule teddy bear and a duplicate. I detached the spare key and used it to lock the caravan door behind me: the original I left as a tantalizing puzzle.

My parting gift to the detectives would be a classic "locked room mystery".

Chapter Ten

THE BAKER'S TALE

As soon I left I did something I had never done before. Instead of hoping that my crime would remain undiscovered, preferably for ever, I did what I could to expedite exposure. My main approach was an anonymous 'phone call.

In this instance I could not leave his body to rot, much as I might like to. Time was of the essence if his associates were to be brought to account. Suspicions would be aroused if his customers were deprived of their regular diet of corruption. It would not take long for them to be scattered to the winds: the birds would have flown. It amazes me when insanity is used as a plea for the most horrendous crimes. To my simple mind anyone who has the intelligence to avoid detection and escape justice is not mad! Just evil.

Bearing all this in mind I didn't even wait to get home. I pulled into an out of town superstore car park and used a public telephone. The crowds and bustle somehow gave me a comforting sense of anonymity. Once more I employed my vocal skills. This time in the impersonation of a young child, gender didn't matter. In fact the less specific the better.

I decided against a direct approach, so it wasn't the police I rang but a child protection agency. I kept the message brief but succinct. In a distraught voice, slightly higher than my normal pitch, I mimicked the tone of a frightened child. I gave the tale of a friend who had been abducted to a derelict caravan, but had escaped and managed to remember details of its location. I knew that they may believe her – they may not, but they could not afford to ignore the plea.

That done I went home and unloaded the car. I emptied the backpack onto my dining table, and for a few minutes just stared at it as if mesmerised. In fact I was thinking about disposal. It seemed a waste, but it was a ticking time bomb, but how to defuse it? Total destruction was the only solution: harder said than done to obliterate the contents of any hard drive.

The hardware casing could be smashed easily enough but the software was another matter and that contained the evidence of my existence: the data. I needed to separate one from the other. A quick computer refresher course was in order. So I fired up my laptop and did a little research. With less than the delicate skill of a surgeon I took a hammer to the unit and removed its heart: the hard drive. A high powered magnet is probably one of the best resolutions, but lacking this I resorted to my limited supply of power tools. Following internet advice I donned some safety glasses and gloves and took a sander to the drive platters. Job done. All the components disappeared into the land fill section of the local recycling plant.

With the removal of the last tiny piece of plastic I tried to settle back into routine. Another first: I didn't even bother to follow media reports. All I wanted was to forget, but like the annihilation of the hard drive – easier said than done.

No remorse came to haunt me: no Shakespearean phantoms disturbed my slumbers. But that bedroom I could not forget. What my eyes hadn't seen my imagination filled in. I could not visit, or contact Emma, without images of what would have been her fate.

Even our old shared pastime provided no escape. It was impossible not to see my console without remembering a similar one and its surroundings. I would still play, but mainly to divert Emma and restore her confidence. She was too young to be tainted with fear: as long as she kept a healthy scepticism about no longer accepting statement as fact.

For myself, I had learnt all about the harsh realities of life. I could no longer go online without feeling exposed to all perils of the planet. In ancient days, when the written word was the only non verbal form of communication, there were warnings placed on maps. The edges of the known world carried the caution "Here there be monsters". Nowadays we have undefined limits and when we cross those we should remember that advice.

Many years previously, when I was still young in body and outlook I suffered a bout of depression. Not the manic variety, now termed "bipolar," but clinical depression, or now MDD (major depression disorder). In "mild" manifestations it is a persistent feeling of sadness. In my case it was a slough of despair. It has been described as a blip on the emotional graph. Normally we drift happily along riding the crests and troughs of life. When depression hits we sink into a trough and are trapped between the waves of a perfect storm. It is a terminal condition, since although we can usually ride it out, as long as there are highs and lows we are always in danger of relapse.

My old adversary decided to pay a return visit. Hardly a surprise. Emotionally and psychologically I was at a low ebb. Believe it or not, I am a natural optimist, but the world had become an alien place. I was struggling to find any joy in it. All of this, and I was so, so tired.

Then fate threw me a life line. As it happened I was overdue for my annual visit north. My aunt was expecting me and sent an invitation in the form of a letter. The overriding symptom of depression is apathy, and it took every ounce of my mental and physical strength to make the effort of a response.

I hardly remember the exhausting drive, but I will always treasure the memory of my gentle aunt. She had not reached her advanced age without being able to recognise melancholy when she saw it. A sixth sense, finely honed over eight decades of experience, provided treatment. She was wise enough to know that the one thing you do not do is suggest the glib cure "pull yourself together."

Instead she set about nudging me out into the world, beginning by a walk to our old friend Gladys. I hardly recognised the person from my last visit. Medication alone could not have brought about such a positive change. Here was a truly happy and content person. A transformation, I suddenly realised, partially brought about by my actions.

So began my recovery. Certain things they say you never forget: like riding a bike, but sometimes you need training wheels. Aunt Dot provided those until I remembered that, along with the villains in this world, there are also heroes. Instead of seeing only the former, I began noticing the latter.

They were still out there, and you find them in the most unlikely places, in the most successful disguises.

At the end of my visit I arranged a morale boosting trip to the hairdresser. If nothing else it would wash out the last remnants of blue rinse. It was during this session that I found a kindred spirit. OK, maybe not a mass murderer, but certainly a vigilante to a lesser degree.

During treatment I caught a conversation between my neighbouring patron and her confidante. What made me prick up my ears was that this was not the usual mutual gripe between client and stylist. It began with the declaration that "well I couldn't just sit back could I". Intrigued, I managed to overhear the following tale, while somehow maintaining my own salon chair conversation. No easy feat, especially since it all took place in a broad Yorkshire dialect.

The narrator I saw reflected in the mirror was a grandmother. A 'butter wouldn't melt' type of woman: we were probably contemporaries. Her story revealed another aspect of society: malice is not the prerogative of grown ups. In this case school bullying had been the source of her grandson's misery.

She handled the problem in a typically no nonsense manner, and described it with the blunt candour I love in that part of the country. A sensible, and successful, solution; although probably not humane and definitely not legal. But maybe that just depends on your viewpoint. Certainly it was no joke to the bullies, but it provided satisfaction to her grandson, and entertainment for her audience. Since the whole tale was related with natural northern dour humour. If laughter is indeed the best medicine, then I was in for a miracle cure.

In a way it begins with our old friends, the seven deadly sins. Although in this case it would not prove lethal. But the harmful effects of bullying should never be underestimated or ignored. It too often leads to the ultimate escape on the part of its prey. Gluttony may be classified as one of the lesser sins, but like any other addiction it may lead to worse temptations.

But I will commence where this rational woman did – at the beginning. Every school day her grandson was accosted by a trio of boys who picked through his lunch and removed the choicest morsels. This culinary mugging was accompanied by mainly verbal abuse, with the occasional push or shove thrown in.

There was little consolation for the boy in the fact that he was not alone. These three wannabe thugs were the bane of their class, and conducted daylight robbery on a strictly democratic basis. No-one's lunch was safe. There appeared to be no excuse for this behaviour. None of the bullies were under nourished, but neither were they fat. Their home lives were healthy and functional with attentive and generous parents. But perhaps therein lay the problem. Power without responsibility, and we all know who finds work for idle hands. Whatever the cause, the result was misery for their class mates.

As most abused children will, the boy did his best to hide his embarrassment. Grandparents, grandmothers in particular, have a built in radar for any deviations from normal behaviour and are not easily deceived. Grandmothers could also teach the Gestapo some interrogation skills, where the truth is extracted via compassion rather than pliers. My salon companion soon wheedled the truth from her increasingly hungry and harassed grandson.

Silence is the secret collaborator of the bully. Once broken half the battle is won. She encouraged the boy to share the open secret with his fellow victims. Up until now they had been intimidated into a regime of divide and conquer. In the meantime the grandmother worked at her own permanent solution.

An opportunity came up in the form of a school coach trip. Normally this would be an occasion for excited anticipation. An outing under the pretext of extra curriculum activity. But, given the current circumstances, only three pupils were enthusiastic about the prospect. It would extend the scope of their extortion. No longer content with filling their stomachs they were beginning to line their pockets. This excursion would be a perfect opportunity with parents providing pocket money for gifts and snacks.

Unlike many of his friends, Matthew (my narrator's grandson) was provided with a special treat by his grandmother: a homemade chocolate cake. It was a special recipe and would have been irresistible to his class mates. Had it not been stolen by the greedy threesome almost as soon as he boarded the coach.

Of course the baker counted on this eventuality. In fact Matthew had had absolutely no intention of sharing the cake with his friends. Any more than he intended eating it himself. He knew that his grandmother's cake mixture included a delicious, but strong, cocoa essence designed to mask the final secret ingredient – laxative!

The woman was very proud of her grandson's amateur

dramatics abilities. Somehow he managed to continue his role as "victim", all the while restraining a smirk of satisfaction. He watched as the self appointed leader of his tormentors triumphantly carried the prize back to his cohorts. The boy strutted to the rear of the coach, where his group had commandeered the coveted rear seats.

He could not wait to show off his spoils and soon the sound of laughter was muffled by rowdy consumption of the booty. Matthew sank down in his own seat. While outwardly giving the impression of utter despair, inside he was jumping for joy. The element of subterfuge added an extra thrill. He was the one in control. The fact that everyone else remained in ignorance of this detail just increased the pleasure.

At the same time he hoped that the effects of the medication would hold off until they were safely on their way. Despite everything he was looking forward to this excursion.

Officially the trip was a geographical exercise to study the cliffs on the north east coast. But most cliffs, by their nature, end at a shoreline. Now an outing to the seaside was a completely different kettle of fish (pun fully intended). For this exciting opportunity all the students gladly put up with the inevitable geological lecture and subsequent homework.

This buoyant mood even infected the teachers: who were young graduates and therefore not, in years, much senior to their pupils. After the obligatory teaching session, they rejoined the coach and made for the nearest resort. It was past lunch time, but free time found everyone making a mass invasion of the nearest fish and chip shop.

Fish and chips always tastes different at the seaside,

maybe because of the belief that the cod or haddock is fresh. Likewise eating it from paper, rather than china plates, adds to the gastronomical enjoyment. All these benefits were discussed over lunch – with far more enthusiasm than the spectacular cliffs.

Many of Matthew's more vulnerable class mates had not only been relieved of their packed lunches but also their funds. This would have made the seaside a less fulfilling experience, except for his grandmother's foresight. She had secreted enough paper money in his rucksack to feed the entire class if need be. The bullies were so pleased to find the cake they had overlooked the hidden stash. They may have wondered why everyone was tucking into a hearty meal – except by now they had other worries.

While the coach driver waited a roll call was made. Coach drivers must acquire saintly patience, since in my experience there are always at least two passengers who can be relied upon to return late. To add insult to injury they usually saunter back, seemingly oblivious to the annoyance of their fellow travellers. In this instance there were three absentees.

After a delay of ten minutes the trio shuffled back. They looked a little green around the gills and somewhat hesitant in their movements. There was absolutely no sympathy from the teachers, who were becoming tired and short tempered.

The coach had no conveniences and the journey back took twice as long due to several unscheduled stops. You can only be grateful that you have to imagine rather than experience the atmosphere in that coach. Fortunately some of the teachers carried spray deodorants, but it was a close vote which odour was the most nauseating. Strangely enough it was always the same three desperate boys who made their cheek clenching totter from the rear of the coach at every halt.

With every delay the driver and teachers became more tetchy. In comparison the children found that laughter is a good antidote for fear. It is very hard to feel intimidated by someone who clearly has failed to reach the nearest bush in time.

What made it all the more perfect was that instead of commiseration in their shared misery, the fellow sufferers were squabbling. Wretched as they were it still seemed essential to apportion blame. Words were said in anger which could never be taken back. The unholy trinity was dissolved by the time the coach arrived home.

The boys soon recovered, but their reputation did not. The combination of isolation with ridicule was fatal, at least for the bullies. Their reign of terror was well and truly over. Unfortunately for them the memory of their disgrace was not so easily erased. It became the stuff of folklore and was passed on from one school year to the next. The retelling would provide laughter for years to come.

It certainly made us laugh. As the story progressed it drew more attention, until at its conclusion the whole salon shared the humour. It was the first time in a long while that I had enjoyed such pure, liberating mirth.

Once the laughter had died down a question came from the audience: "But why didn't you go to the authorities?" The reply was considered but brief "Yes, but it wouldn't have been so satisfying."

Not only must Justice be done, it must also be seen to be done.

Chapter Eleven

THE BOOKMAN'S TALE

A few days later I bid goodbye to my aunt and returned home, a happier and much wiser woman. With every intention to turn back a leaf and end my vigilante activities.

It was high summer, and after an uneventful trip to Wales, I returned with my resolution still intact. Putting my old life behind me I didn't even check to see if anything had been dragged from a slurry pit.

All was going well, probably too well, when I accepted the invitation of a reunion with some former work colleagues. Always a mixed blessing to catch up with people from our past. There will always be people better or worse off than yourself.: inciting equal amounts of envy and conceit. Added to which each successive reunion brings with it the reminder of your own mortality. As you grow older the members grow fewer.

There are always some people you tend to avoid at such gatherings. Unfortunately these individuals are like cats, who seem instinctively to gravitate to those who do not like them. On the other hand, those whom you are genuinely glad to see are usually hard to find: possibly because they are surrounded by friends.

At this particular event I searched for one such colleague, and there he was, the same larger than life character. John, a commissioning editor of the old school, was delightfully eccentric and old fashioned in manner and dress. He was also an increasingly rare commodity in business – a real gentleman.

He looked the same as ever, in his flannel jacket and panama hat. He didn't even look much older and it had been three years since I had last seen him. As I have learnt to my cost, the ageing process speeds up along with the number of your birthdays. No, physically he hadn't changed, but there was something wrong.

After the usual pleasantries I thought to cheer him up by recounting the story of the school bullies. We shared a similar sense of humour but knew I had hit a raw nerve when he commented " not all tyrants are in the classroom". He then confided to me the reason for his unusual dejection.

It seemed that he had recently run foul of an obnoxious individual. A man in a position of power, but lacking any morals or sense of responsibility. A man so consumed with self importance as to be utterly devoid of any compassion. In fact a man the polar opposite to John.

An arrogant man, accurately described in the poet Dante's definition of pride as "love of self, perverted to hatred and contempt of one's neighbour."

The concept of pride for me has always been an uneasy concoction of vice and virtue. It is a sin, but it is so often celebrated. Our society urges us to take pride in our children, work, achievements, and even appearance.

But pride in Christian terms is an offence against God. A form of self worship which gives no reverence or respect to our Creator. No wonder that in many theological circles it is regarded as the cardinal sin: the source from which all others flow. None of us are free from some form of self pride, which makes it the more deadly.

For centuries governments have found this human flaw extremely useful and exploited it to full advantage.

The ideals of democracy may have been advocated since ancient times, but in practice our rulers have found it convenient to implement "divide and rule" regimes.

In Roman times it was the Christians who found themselves at the sharp end of this strategy. "Bread and circuses" historically has been a tactic employed to pacify the "mob" and provide scapegoats for their frustration and anger. It still is. There is one problem with this as far as we "the rabble" are concerned. One moment we are sitting in the audience, part of the crowd; the next we are in the arena.

I have certainly learnt that lesson since retirement. No longer a valued individual, I am now relegated to the ranks of the expensive nuisance. More commonly known as pensioners.

How far is it from being a nuisance to being expendable. Not far – just a step. You only have to go back over the past 80 years to prove this. The deadly combination of pride and prejudice has led to the subjugation and annihilation of millions on the basis of fabricated cultural, religious, and racial superiority.

Now I was beginning to understand why pride, as perverted self esteem, is such a dangerous and subversive weapon.

In any job where there are elements of money and control you will find your fair share of self serving hypocrites. Of course there are also sincere individuals who have not abandoned their religious or humanitarian ideals. But power corrupts and it takes a strong conscience to withstand temptation.

Politics is one such occupation. You don't have to walk the hallowed halls of Westminster to become a casualty of your own spin. There are town and county halls around the country which testify to the failure of good intentions.

Of course some people never even begin with good intentions, they arrive as fully formed egotists. Such individuals forget, if they ever knew, that they were elected to serve their communities and not their own ends.

With this observation I have come full circle back to my friend, John, and his problem. An irritating pain in the arse which took the form of a local councillor.

John had run foul of this bureaucrat by doing what he should have and standing up for the more vulnerable members of his constituency. There is one typical quality about pride: it cannot tolerate criticism. When this censure is public the repercussions can be extreme.

Through the old boys network this individual had made John's life a living Hell. He admitted that it had become so bad he had seriously considered moving away. John, being John, however he still put his harassed neighbours before personal comfort or safety.

But he confided to me that he was now forced to review that decision. The situation, which had began with unpleasant fabricated rumours against John's character, had advanced to veiled threats against his property and even family.

That's probably why my story about the bullied

schoolboy rang such a bell. Bullies, if not dealt with at school, carry their destructive behaviour with them. If lucky this is restricted to the workplace, if not, as in this case, there are no limits. John had tried to check this despot, but as with my Yorkshire schoolboy, he had his own gang of fellow creeps. Perhaps I could learn a lesson from that anecdote – divide and conquer.

It was hard to see such a strong and decent person so desperate. Maybe I would come out of retirement for a while.

Then for some reason I remembered an old saying of my grandmother's:-

"If you have a friend then keep them so, but NEVER let your friend your secrets know. For when your friend becomes your foe, then where do all your secrets go?"

Those who live by the sword die by the sword: although this instance I didn't intend anything so drastic. For sword read media: they have something in common, they are both double edged. My opponent wouldn't be the first person to manipulate publicity, nor would he be the first to realise that the presses, once put in motion, are difficult to control.

This I recognised could be his downfall, but I needed ammunition. I knew one thing for sure: I needed no disguise. This obnoxious individual was so blinkered in attitude that he would never see me at all. Just another female: and one old enough to be of no interest or use.

Feeling a bit like Miss Marple, I nosed around and found out more about his business activities. He ran a small printing firm, which appeared completely above board. But I expected that: you have to be extremely lazy and arrogant to crap in your own nest.

However there seemed to be a lot of extra curriculum interests which fell between his private and public roles. Suffice it to say, he had his fingers in enough pies to stock a bakery.

Most people were privately happy to gossip about his activities, but no one was willing to blow a whistle. Quite understandable given the hate campaign conducted against my friend. One thing all my confidantes agreed upon: he was a very bad enemy.

I had no such fears because I wasn't going to approach this problem honestly as my friend had. I was going to sneak around the back door. I took my trusty cell phone and started gathering photographic evidence.

I found plenty of it. I am surprised he had time to attend any meetings given the extent of his wheeler dealing. One thing was certain he didn't waste much time or effort on his voters. No doubt he thought he would have moved on to bigger and better things before the next election.

I was building up my portfolio and in it backhanders featured prominently. Old fashioned, but untraceable, cash transfers from developers, contractors, builders, planning requestors, you name them. Anyone who needed to grease his palms for the right results. Bad enough, but often these decisions, far from defending his constituents rights, made their lives more wretched.

So for the next weeks, as autumn once more crept towards us, I collected a dossier of information. All of his transactions corroborated by photographs. It soon became obvious that he was so conceited he thought he was untouchable. He had obviously never heard of the old adage about pride and fall.

All was complete, but I bided my time until the arrival of the silly season." Traditionally the end of summer when the newspapers have a sparse time and are desperate for news. The more shocking the better. The apples were ripe for plucking and I had a few select rotten ones ready for serving up.

I put together a select, tantalising package, and mailed copies off to the local and national papers. I had no way of knowing how far his network of influence stretched, but I hoped the London journalists would be impartial. It was an anonymous contribution, but there were a few subtle hints.

Among all the images of bribery and corruption I had slipped a few choice snaps of adultery. Oh nothing too explicit, my funds don't stretch to those sort of cameras and lenses. But the spouse featured just happened to be the wife of an associate of my subject. Not exactly a signed admission, but what could be better revenge for cuckolded husband than public humiliation of his rival. The press could draw their own conclusions: they usually do anyway.

As usually if it worked, great, if not no harm done. Either way there was nothing to link the exposÈ to John. Besides I had the feeling that Mr Corrupt Councillor would have more pressing matters on his mind in the very near future.

I was not wrong. Before the trees dropped their leaves the case had become a major sensation. The public love to see idols toppled,especially those who create their own pedestals. As soon as it became clear that the tables had turned, many previously intimidated colleagues stepped forward as witnesses for the prosecution. Of course this also included some of his partners in crime: the phrase "rats" and "sinking ship" come to mind.

I spoke to John when the scandal hit the headlines. It would have seemed strange not to. John has a more generous nature than mine, and his initial comment was one of relief for his neighbours. But he knew me well enough to anticipate my remarks: which were something to the effect "what goes around comes around".

As you have discovered I rarely read newspapers and this was no exception. I took no pleasure from either the media witch hunt, or the subsequent legal proceedings. But I was pleased to learn, from a mutual friend, that John had been persuaded to enter local politics. He would be an excellent advocate and a welcome change from the previous incumbent.

Chapter Twelve

THE PEDLARS TALE

Christmas came and went. I was feeling pretty good about myself. Congratulating myself that I had managed to bring justice without reverting to more direct action. In this I was, of course, guilty of my own pride. I would have done well to remember my own warnings about that.

It seems a bit late at this point to elaborate on the personal details I have so far avoided. But it is important and relevant to this penultimate chapter, so please indulge me.

I still live in the same house in which I was born. Initially I shared this with my maternal grandmother, who brought me up. My father walked away shortly after my birth: my mother waited a couple of years later. At this point a prospective new husband appeared on the horizon, in a westerly direction over the Atlantic. This proved a more successful match, as a result of which there is now an American branch of our family. In fact it is the only limb of our ancestral tree since I have produced no offshoots.

All this, I realise, could be cited as a defence for my recent eccentric behaviour. It is not. My grandmother did an excellent job and I never felt any lack of attention or love.

Just the opposite, as time went on and I rationally thought about my life, I was grateful for its course. Both my parents, unintentionally, provided me with the best mother and tutor imaginable.

The values she instilled in me are nowadays considered old fashioned, even objects of ridicule, but they served generations of our ancestors well enough. Virtues like loyalty, honesty, courtesy were all once part of civilised behaviour. Yet ironically the more we have advanced, the less moral we have become.

My grandmother, and her principles, seem to have long departed this earth. While I miss her terribly I am glad she is not here to witness what has become of the brave new world.

Anyway that is my potted personal history. For many years now I have lived alone, but not lonely. Most of that time I have shared my hopes and fears with Jean, my neighbour. A therapy session usually conducted over a soothing cup of tea and some of her home baked goodies.

Of course, I have never taken anyone into my confidence as far as my nefarious activities are concerned. Least of all a treasured friend: that would be an unfair burden and not part of my promise to protect the innocent. So for my darkest thoughts I keep my own counsel.

But it was a bright January morning and I thought that part of my life was well and truly over. I had come through the last test with my resolve more or less in tact. Judgement and punishment I had left to society's guardians. Okay I had given them a little push, but isn't that what a law abiding citizen does. My only problem now was to try and put the past behind me. Time, the great healer, may even be able to consign my guilty memories to the status of a bad dream.

Later that day, after the daily household chores, Jean and I were sharing tea and sympathy. As usual our gripes and moans ranged the whole gambit from personal problems to "putting the world to rights."

Being the same age, class and gender, our conversations were mainly mutual commiseration rather than discussion. You could say it was a very compact support network. It is comforting to unburden yourself to someone who is guaranteed not only to understand your predicament, but reinforce your solution.

Jean had just produced a freshly baked tray of biscuits, and a second cuppa, as our agenda reached its halfway point. We had dealt with all our individual joys and sorrows, and now moved on to local concerns.

Immediately I could sense a change in my confidante. A body language expert would have had a field day with her gestures. I knew very little about the skill, but nervous hands are a dead giveaway. My friend's agitated hands were sending clear signals that this was not a routine anxiety. Even her voice noticeably dropped, in tone and volume, to a whisper.

It was bleak winter's day, but we were sitting in a comfortable, warm kitchen. Nevertheless her mood was contagious: despite the cosy atmosphere, I began to feel anxious and chilly. The situation she went on to describe did nothing to dispel that atmosphere.

She began by explaining that a few weeks ago new neighbours had moved into the rental property next door. Truthfully I had not noticed their arrival, but said nothing. I did not want to disrupt her train of thought, or interrupt her narrative. I had the strong feeling that this emotionhad already been pent up too long and the best treatment was release.

At first the tenants seemed like a typical small family: husband, wife and toddler. With a contrasting mixture of natural courtesy and southern reserve, my friend offered her usual welcome. A bottle of wine and home baked cake. Having delivered her house warming gift she returned to her home, with every intention of minding her own business.

Jean was probably the least curious person I knew. She valued her own privacy too much to intrude into the lives of others. Like most of our generation she kept her lace nets, but she used them as security not ascreen to spy on her neighbours. There was no curtain twitching in our windows. But all this was about to change.

She went on to explain that it was becoming impossible to ignore the nocturnal comings and goings which centred around the new residents. This nightly routine commenced within a couple of days, and continued with the regularity of the proverbial clockwork. The disturbance was caused, not by human vocal cords, but traffic.

Every night cars would arrive at 10pm, park for a few minutes and then drive off. This lasted for approximately half an hour. At least this inconvenience was confined to the sound of car engines and the reflected glare of headlamps. If they talked it was muted, and there was no noise of doors slamming. No one apparently left or entered the vehicles. All then went quiet until 4am when the process would be repeated.

In the first week, while this was still an unwelcome novelty, Jean lay in bed watching the headlight beams slide across her bedroom ceiling. She consoled herself with the idea that these were probably teething troubles, and adopted a policy of understanding tolerance. I thought, as I listened to her, that this was a fatal error. I have learnt, to my own cost, that accepting the thin end of the wedge is an open invitation for future misery.

I realised, as she was talking, that I had been a neglectful friend. Not until this moment had I noticed how tired she had become. Now I belatedly recognised the telltale signs of extended fatigue: dark deep circles around her eyes. The reason for this became clear as she described how the sleepless nights turned into sleepless weeks. At our time of life an uninterrupted night's rest is never taken for granted, and once awoken there is no guarantee of a swift return to the arms of Morpheus. Fortunately she had managed to catch a few winks during the day when all went quiet next door, but this upheaval was creating havoc with her body clock.

A change of bedrooms had only temporarily helped. By now she had become such a light sleeper she was awake at the slightest noise. A week ago she admitted she was close to taking the ultimate step of self medication, when another event overtook that decision.

She had taken to going to bed either earlier in the evening, or after 10.30pm, in the hope of at least avoiding the 10 o'clock commotion. On this particular night she had taken the 9pm option. This turned out to be so successful that she was enjoying a rare dream when she was jerked back into reality.

It took her a brief moment to adjust her senses to their location and become aware of the cause of her rude awakening. As she still struggled between the inclination to sleep and consciousness, the sound of raised voices forced her fully back into the land of the living. She glanced at the clock, which provided the only light source in the room, and blinked, it was 4.10am! Then her eyes went to the illumination coming through the . gap in the bedroom curtains. Instinctively, she was drawn to this light. She did what she had avoided so far: she got out of bed and went to the window. Still following this unusual impulse, she stood back behind the curtains and peeked out. Safely protected by the thick winter drapes, and the darkness, she watched events outside.

There was obviously an argument going on between her new male neighbour and the driver of a parked car. The latter seemed to be reluctant to hand over something he withheld in his left hand. After this heated discussion continued for a further five minutes, there appeared to be some resolution. Finally he appeared satisfied and surrendered the article. The car was parked under the street lamp so it was easy to see the thick wad of money.

I think Jean, although she was unaware of it, already had her suspicions about the nature of her neighbour's business. She had been prepared to give the benefit of the doubt, but knowledge had removed consideration. Now she wanted to know the whole truth.

The next night she sat up in anticipation of the first session of deliveries. 10pm sharp and several vehicles began their visits. Only this time the drivers were not delivering, they were collecting. Harmless enough looking carrier bags but bulging with identically shaped smaller packages.

Sod's law, although she had set the alarm for 3.30am, she

almost overslept. In fact she was just slipping back on the pillows when the first car arrived back. Mentally shaking herself awake she went to the window and watched the returning cavalcade of vehicles. She recognised several of their makes and models. This time though their drivers were handing back shopping bags, but with differently shaped contents.

Here Jean paused, this latest disclosure had brought the situation bang up to date. But I knew she had not finished: something still prayed on her mind. I knew what it was. She was in quandary, but reluctant to speak her suspicions aloud. Somehow if we voice our fears they become real. So instead I put the question as a statement "drug dealers". Even then she gave no answer, except the faintest dip of her head.

I was used to taking matters into my own hands – literally – but drugs are a serious commitment. Drugs, like pride, are the rotten source from which many other evils grow. Their roots are intricate and well established. They are supported and nurtured by dangerous and powerful people. The stakes were too high for me to take this on as a solo venture.

But perhaps I could follow the success of my previous project. A strategy of involved non involvement. I could be a detective without being judge and jury. I would, of course, have to be more careful than ever before, because the felons in this case would make no distinction. They would certainly show no leniency to my age. I recognised too that any personal risks I took must not be transferred to my friend.

Trying not to alarm her I asked Jean if she had spoken to anyone else about her neighbours. She said not and I believed her. There is something so menacing about drugs and their dealers which intimidates everyone into silence. It is a deliberate and well honed practice since it makes their life easier. I was not surprised that they had selected such a small quiet location: surrounded by retirees they dismissed as ineffectual. Why not, governments do?

Little did they know, however, what lurked behind my door. If they noticed me at all it was as just another pensioner. For once a useful commodity since I, and my kind, provided cover for their operations. Despite this I was under no illusion of the force of retaliation if that fantasy changed. Even more important that I protect Jean from any potential danger.

But I needed assistance without her being aware she was providing it. So, feeling a little shamefaced, I used my genuine concern for her welfare to make a suggestion. Perhaps it would be a good idea if we house swapped for a few nights to allow Jean to catch up on her sleep. She saw nothing odd in this proposal: we had done so before. All was so easily settled – I could put up with the guilt pangs. We would live in our respective houses as normal, but switch sleeping arrangements at bedtime. This manoeuvre would give Jean the peace she needed, and myself the opportunity for my own R & R: record and reconnoitre.

No better time than the present, so I looked out my trusty backpack and prepared for the evening exchange. At 9 pm we crossed paths and back gardens: luckily there was a deliveries access gate which had never been sealed. I had suggested this would cause less hassle, but it also meantno prying eyes would witness our movements.

I went straight upstairs and set up an observation post.

Unpacking the backpack: pyjamas for appearance's sake; a phone, notebook and binoculars for necessity's. I dragged a chair – comfortable, but not seductive – to the window. All was now ready, except one final item – a flask of coffee. It is not a beverage I normally drink, but it does have certain stimulating qualities. Everything was in position by 9.50pm. I didn't have to wait long – according to Jean's account, my first visitor arrived early. So began my vigil. Every vehicle's registration was logged along with make, model and colour. The last proved difficult since street lamps are notoriously inaccurate in this respect. It was not reliable, but with my written records it didn't need to be. On realisation of this fact I decided to abandon the idea of photography. It was pointless: the phone quality would not provide any useful additional evidence, and it was not worth the risk of an incriminating flash. I tried to disable this function, but had a lack of faith in technology and my abilities to control it.

The phone was not a complete waste of time. Among its other uses, apart from communications, was a vibrating alarm. This allowed me to snatch a nap between sessions. I had set the wake up tremble for 3.30pm, so had a short wait before the first headlights appeared. It was the same vehicle which led the first parade. Efficiency must have been the driver's one virtue, of so many vices.

My second stint was slightly different from the earlier. Whereas I had initially recorded details, now I used this list to cross off the returning vehicles. I counted everyone of them back. By the time the last straggler dropped off their "shopping" it was almost five. This was my normal "first cuppa" time, so I went downstairs and helped myself to Jean's supplies. Everything had been placed in plain view, except the milk, including a plate of homemade biscuits. I took my booty back to bed, where I barely had time to consume it before I fell asleep. When I next dragged myself into consciousness the clock read eight fifteen.

We had given no morning rendezvous time: allowing nature to do its best, but I thought Jean would be up by now. So I dragged myself and gear back through the gate. In any case I had a spare key for the rear door, so I would not disturb my guest. As it turned out our internal clocks must have been set in tandem because I found her drinking tea in the kitchen. She looked a very different person from the one I had last seen. Amazing what a good night's sleep can do.

We shared a second pot of tea, along with our comparative nights. Maintaining my fiction, I lied through my teeth and said that I had slept soundly. I knew that if I gave any hint of tiredness she would refuse to keep to our agreement. Jean needed more than one night's recuperation, and I needed more surveillance time. As it was, I am ashamed to say, she believed me and we both got what we wanted.

That night we repeated the exercise, except this time I added one more item to my pack. I had an old digital camera, which had been recently neglected. It was not so ancient however that it did not have night vision. So with this fully charged I took up my usual window seat and filmed every vehicle, zooming in and out on its driver.

With this done on the first shift, I crashed out on the ample sofa downstairs for the rest of the night. I may have managed quite well upstairs on the bed, but could not risk looking exhausted in the morning. I had to keep up the pretence a little longer for Jean's sake. For myself, I now had everything I needed.

What to do next? Well, apart from the fact that I would be out of my depth dealing with such a large and well organised group, I still had my renewed faith in authority. So I did what any normal member of society would do – I went to the police. OK I'll admit that with a body count of five to my credit, I was hardly a candidate for a citizen of the year award.

Early the next day I went along to my local police station and found it closed. I was surprised since it had been a major operational base built in the 1960s to police the growing suburbs. These same suburbs had since grown to the point of over development, but were obviously under funded. A notice stated that the building was no longer manned on a 24 hour basis, and provided an emergency number. Not much consolation or protection if I had been chased here by a knife wielding maniac! I felt a slight blip on my radar of confidence.

I walked back home, and had a cup of tea with my oblivious neighbour. That was the way I wanted it to remain. She had no idea of my mission and I had no intention of enlightening her. It is very often an incorrect assumption, but I felt in this case "what she did not know could not hurt her".

This delay gave me time to think, and my thoughts now tended to an indirect approach. What if my neighbours, or their accomplices, had seen me outside the police station? Probably not: they would have been safely tucked up in bed by then. Even if they had I doubt they would recognise me. I had not previously known of their existence, why would they notice mine? But it was a lesson well learnt and I decided instead to make a telephone approach.

Later that morning I rang the local constabulary, and miraculously was immediately connected to a living being instead of the usual automaton. She was operating a sort of police triage system, and asked what was the nature of my problem. After a brief summary, I was advised of my transferral to an officer in the Drug Squad.

This time a male voice answered and introduced himself, although I doubt many people actually register this information. Perhaps I am in the minority, but I seldom record, let alone remember, the names of telephone contacts. In this case it was different, the call was not about malfunctioning services, but a highly dangerous gang of criminals. I was trusting this man with privileged information and possibly my life.

Bearing this in mind, and carefully omitting any reference to Jean, I went into the more detailed account I had rehearsed. At points I was forced to pause and elaborate on certain facts. One of them was a visual description of the tenants. As it happened I could do better than that. During Jean's welcome attempt, which in the narrative became mine, an introduction had included the family's Christian names. It soon became clear that both parents were well known to the police. In fact the husband was a personal "thorn in the side" to their department. An elusive character who somehow managed to slip through any net they cast, leaving just the small fry. These unlucky dealer users were usually just as much victims as their clients. The wife and mother, in her turn, was an old acquaintance of the vice squad. Young as she was, she had a long and colourful history as a prostitute.

With this knowledge any regrets that I may have had

regarding the future welfare of their child vanished. I could only feel sorry for the present situation of the little girl, and wish her out of their influence as soon as possible. Almost any upbringing would better and safer than her current existence. There has been a lot of negative publicity about foster care, but I have known many generous and loving surrogate parents.

While my mind was digesting all this new information I was aware that I was being asked to make a statement. The last thing I wanted was a police officer, even a plain clothes version, turning up on my doorstep. But I had no time for objections: an alternative suggestion was already offered. I should have given them more credit, of course they were experienced in the ways of drug dealers. They had learnt the hard way never to underestimate the risks involved, not only to themselves and witnesses, but their own families. If I had any remaining delusions about the severity of my involvement they were gone now.

An appointment was made for me to make the statement in a "safe house" – a few miles away in the county police headquarters. I agreed to take any evidence along with me. There was a chilling postscript to this arrangement in that I should use public transport where it would be easier to spot any surveillance.

So the next day, the designated date, I set out. Knowing that the circuitous route would involve a three bus transportation, I allowed plenty of time. In my experience such journeys usually follow two routes: either so smoothly that you arrive far too early; or so badly that you are still late. In this instance it was the former: I had plenty of time to spare to investigate the unknown local shops.

Even in this innocuous activity I felt vulnerable. There was none of the usual pleasure, or distraction, in the assortment of independent shops Normally I find these a delightful commercial oasis: a welcome alternative to the standard high street monopolies. But the time passed without my shopping bag growing heavier, or my wallet lighter, and it was time to make my way to the interview.

As I approached my destination caution grew to paranoia, which was only relieved by the faint humour of the situation. I felt like an escapee from some old "B" feature spy film. Those last steps into the police station were made with many double take backward glances. Every fellow pedestrian and motorist became potential threats.

The station reception desk provided no relief, if anything I became more alert to my surroundings, or rather the people within them. It was only when I was ushered into the inner sanctum that I relaxed. By the time I met my contact I was calm enough for another shock. I should have been prepared, after all it was the drug squad. But the officer who now greeted me in the flesh was no one's idea of a policeman. I wondered for a brief moment if, by some bizarre means, a dealer from the street had followed me into the station.

He must have seen my reaction, because when he offered his hand he also gave an apology. Something to the effect that "When you wallow with pigs, you expect to get dirty". To say this was an understatement. But then his safety depended on the complete conviction of his disguise. If he was acting a role then it had to be in the Stanislavski method school. The complete immersion of self into character. It may not win him any academy awards, but it might keep him alive.

Formalities over, he led me into an office. From the personal affects, although not to the point of including photographs, I gathered that this was his own space. I don't know what I expected, a bare interview room probably, based on too many police shows. I was shown to a comfortably upholstered chair across a desk from his own. He offered a tea or coffee, and while I selected the former, he moved his seat closer. While he left the room, I assumed to procure the drinks, I had time to reflect on this psychology. The altered seating arrangements were no doubt an attempt to remove the confrontation aspect – to put me at my ease.

It worked. On his return, carrying actual china mugs instead of the taste polluting polystyrene, we sat down to share a surprisingly palatable tea. A few seconds later one of his colleagues, well I assume it wasn't an ageing hippie dragged in off the streets, brought in a plate of biscuits. The feeling of comfort was fading slightly: I was beginning to feel a little like a fatted calf being prepared for sacrifice.

Then we got down to business. First up was the paperwork and then I presented my "evidence". I breathed a silent sigh of relief: well that was my duty done. I was just preparing to make my farewells and leave when the bomb dropped. It was not over. The detective inspector, for such he was, remained glued to his chair and made no effort to move. He was obviously hesitating – perhaps considering the right persuasive tack. I was right in my reservations: the tea and sympathy approach had been a tactical ambush.

I was annoyed: partially through fear, partially through stupidity. After setting so many traps myself, I had fallen into someone else's. At the end of the day there was no choice, I had made my decision once I opted to pass this information to the police. If I was angry it was because I had handed over control of the situation, and myself, to a third party. In case you have not guessed by now, I do not like to feel dependant on others. As it was to turn out all my instincts were perilously accurate in this respect.

Anyway the long and short of it was that the time for excuses was over: so I listened to my "handler" and agreed to his proposal. In effect this was to do what I had done so far: keep a log of the comings and goings at the suspect's property. But there was a difference: for the next week I was to keep watch during the day. Specifically between the hours of three and five p.m. I was intrigued, but mine not to reason why, and at least I would catch up on lost sleep.

Next week Jean would return to her own bed and I would transfer the more limited surveillance to own house. This suited me: I did not want to incriminate my neighbour by providing information that only she was, quite literally, in a position to witness. So I returned home more paranoid than ever, and began my assignment. I learnt quickly something which I had neglected with my emphasis on night time observation. All was quiet during the day until late afternoon, when I took up my post at the front bedroom window. Of course this was more restricted, but still provided a clear view of the pavement and street.

Three o'clock came and went. The only sign of human life was the daily school run, using our road as a shortcut. This convoy of people carriers was, to a lesser degree, supplemented by a few hardy foot travellers. At first this procession would be mainly primary school children, attended by their mothers and younger siblings in pushchairs. Later these were superseded by groups of secondary pupils ranging eleven years old and up. Anyway old enough to recognise it was no longer "cool" to be seen in public with your parent.

By five pm this latter category was reduced to small groups of stragglers: mainly now of the teenage variety. I was preparing to shut down operations for the day, while questioning the wisdom of my task, when I saw something which made me stop.

A group of three boys had been walking up the pavement, but now suddenly disappeared into the drive which I knew to be my target's property. Everything now fell into place: it all made complete sense. Only one thing was wrong: I had been anticipating traffic, not pedestrians. The right time, but wrong place. Tomorrow I would shift operations to the rear.

The implications of the brief glimpse I had seen, provided another restless night. It wasn't that I was shocked, or even surprised – perhaps a little disappointed. No, the reason for my insomnia was adrenaline. I wanted to get on with it: I had wasted a day already. These people needed to be removed from society as soon as possible. If it was my old self that removal would have been permanent, as it was prison would have to suffice.

The next day passed painfully slowly, although I filled some of the hours by selecting my best vantage point. From the experience yesterday I guessed that any exchange would take place from the side door to the property. My own fencing provided a security screen, which was a bonus for them, but a problem for me. The rear windows were useless: hemmed in by my neighbour's extension, they provided no visual access. There was but one alternative: my attic window. On the plus side, no one would notice me looking down from above. On the minus, the ladder access made the setting up procedure murder on my knee caps.

Several hours, and many burnt calories later, all was ready. As previously nothing much happened until around five. When the boys finally came into view I felt almost sick with tension. They were chattering away excitedly: perhaps too much to be entirely natural. Possibly they had been sampling the goods? As I guessed they stopped outside the back door and put down their backpacks. Almost immediately the door opened and there stood our loving husband and father.

The laughter disappeared and all became business. The boys extracted familiar looking carrier bags from their packs and took turns to hand these over. Even with binoculars I could not to see what they received in return – the contents were concealed in envelopes. Once the transaction was complete, and both parties left, I made a telephone call. My contact seemed satisfied, much more than I was. As far as he was concerned I would continue as before. For myself, had already made up my mind on another course of action.

That route led me the next day, at a slightly earlier time, to the gates of the local secondary school. Afternoon break on a cold winter's day and all the pupils having been forced out into the invigorating air. One teacher, or aide, had drawn the short straw and was on playground duty. A responsibility conducted half heartedly from the shelter of a doorway. Most pupils were huddled together in warming groups. One gathering, however, stood out from the others. For one thing it was positioned just out of sight from the supervisory adult. For another it was more energetic. Unlike the other clusters, who basically stood shivering together, this resembled the animation of traders on the stock exchange. Business was obviously being done, but I had the sensation that these were not budding entrepreneurs dealing in stocks and shares.

I lifted the 'phone as if to make or answer a call. but actually took a picture of the group. But I had misjudged the freezing teacher, who was not so laid back as I thought, because she was making a beeline towards me. I had my cover story ready and prepared to take full advantage of my usual allies – age and gender.

Before she reached me, and without giving her the opportunity to speak, I took the offensive. Remembering that the best form of defence is attack, I pre-empted her question with one of my own. "What time does school finish?" Without allowing for interruption I went on to explain that my daughter had asked if I could collect my grandson. I carried on playing the confused geriatric card for all it was worth: waffling on about forgetting the time – blah, blah, blah.

It worked. She was either overwhelmed by my prattle or the cold, and furnished me with details of the school's timetable. Thankfully she never had time to enquire further into my non existent grandchild: I was saved by the recall bell. All her charges were heading back to the comfort of their last classes of the day, and I used this distraction to make my escape.

As far as I was concerned this had now reached new levels of urgency. Without waiting another minute, let alone day, I hit dial on my one of my few saved numbers. The response was for caution and patience, but I had had enough of all this cloak and dagger. I wanted this operation shut down as soon as possible, so I aimed beneath the belt. "Do you have any children?" I asked – the hesitation in his answer told me all I needed to know, including the fact that I had won the argument.

He had one last request: in exchange for this he gave his promise that one more night would see the end to this charade . Again it was a break with former routine, and took me back to night watch. But this time I would not lose much sleep: just from 3.30 until 6 am. In addition there would be one more change: throughout this period a drug squad officer would remain at the other end of an open 'phone line. Every time a vehicle left the premises I would pass on its registration. I asked no further questions, figuring that ignorance is bliss.

So that night I began my final stretch. I slept, what I like to think, the sleep of the just, until 3 am, when I rose and opened up the connection. The answering voice was not my usual contact. He introduced himself as a Detective Constable Smith, I suppose someone has to be, but somehow I doubted this, suspecting fabrication. The rank was probably true: it was a much younger tone, with a distinctive Cockney accent. No doubt a new recruit, confined to desk duty: my regular liaison officer had other, more pressing, matters tonight.

Business must be slow. The first car didn't arrive until 4.15 am., but then there followed a steady stream of traffic. Familiarity breeds contempt and the drivers were no longer subtle about their dealings. This arrogance was evidenced by the raised voices and liberal use of car horns. It was so bad at one point that I was forced to shout through the car numbers. From my associate at the other end, I heard the exclamation "what the bloody hell is going on there?" Judging that it was not the moment for wit or sarcasm, I told the truth.

This Bedlam continued until 5.15am when it finally tailed off and quiet once more descended on the neighbourhood. I gave it another ten minutes before asking the hopeful question "Is that it now?" My receiver picked up some muted discussion, before a request was passed on "could you hold just a little longer?"

Now my curiosity was aroused – what were they waiting for? That question was answered twenty long minutes later. The street was silent and so was the dark car which slowly drove into vision. It was travelling so gently that it did not even brake as it turned into the leased driveway. I lost sight of the vehicle before I could see its plate. An omission which barely mattered, since it was such a distinctive object. I think the term would be high end luxury car – although limousine would probably be more accurate. Whatever the definition, it was ostentation and conceit on four wheels. Somehow I just knew that the missed registration was some personalised affectation. A real naff mobile.

Less than five minutes later I saw the limo gingerly reversing its way out, back onto the highway. Still no opportunity to record its number. But I picked up the 'phone and hoped a description would suffice. Not only was this the case, but my information seemed to produce an audible buzz of celebration. Hardly believing what I was hearing, a voice then ordered "Stand down," before communications were unceremoniously cut. I took me a while to register that this order was directed at me before I pressed my own disconnect button.

Later the next morning, presumably once the dust had settled, I received an apologetic 'phone call from a recognisable voice – my old drug squad associate. His excuse for my treatment was that everyone at the station had been carried away by the excitement of the occasion. He went on to explain, I hoped on a secure line, their strategy. As I had delivered details every member of the gang had followed and picked up. This included the most important catch of the haul, my friend in the limo. This was their leader, a veritable "Mr Big," a notorious, but up until now, elusive criminal. But, to use the vernacular, he had been caught "bang to rights," having been stopped in possession of the spoils of his employees labour. Money and drugs.

Even better, the amount and strength of evidence meant that I would not be required as a witness, always a bonus when you are dealing with a vicious drug baron! No amount of funds could buy a solicitor capable of dodging this charge and conviction.

Although the underling carriers had no clue of their leaders identity, our neighbour obviously did. He had been arrested in the final stages of the operation: so quietly that it had passed under my radar. Or maybe I was just so physically, and emotionally, exhausted that I passed out. Back at the police station, he had been left alone in a stark interview room for all the time necessary to allow him to review his options. Eventually he had seen the error of his ways and sought redemption by turning Queen's evidence against his former boss. A decision encouraged by a guarantee of protection and leniency.

So all's well that ends well – or is it?

On the face of it, yes it was a satisfactory result. A serious criminal was where he should be – safely behind bars, and likely to remain there for the indefinite future. True, there would be no more extra curriculum activity at the local schools for a while: well at least until another parasite surfaced from the swamp of human depravity. The confiscation of the gangster's gas guzzler was another bonus – at least for the planet. This alone, I estimated, would halve carbon emissions.

But, on the down side, my neighbour would be back out on the streets within a few months. Although it was unlikely to be in our area: part of the deal had involved some sort of witness protection scheme. Another successful plea for leniency had been based on his marital status, ironically the very thing which gave me cause for concern. He would return, relocate, and it would be business as usual. What would happen to the little girl? I feared she would disappear into the dregs of society, until she was old enough to earn her keep.

So in my decision to abide by the law, what had happened to my pledge to protect the innocent, as embodied in this baby. What had happened to justice?

This subject became the main topic when Jean and I returned to our regular tea breaks. The hardest part of these discussions was to feign ignorance. It was difficult to continue this pretence with my friend. She didn't know about the prostitution and so she saw the mother as a cause for sympathy. Many of the world's oldest profession are indeed victims, but not so in this case. Between herself and her partner I would be hard pressed to name which was the accomplice.

I tried all I could to divert Jean's attention towards the child. But without opening the can of worms which was my secret life, it was no good. There would be no rest until she had offered her support and help. I could not dissuade her, so I did the only thing left: I agreed to go with her. If she insisted on being the good Samaritan then I would make sure she was not alone. I thought that I knew what I was walking into. As it turned out we were both pitifully naive.

It was a surprisingly bright, warm afternoon: a good omen, if you believe in such things. In fact it was a false Spring, a deception when nature is fooled into awakening prematurely. Perhaps that was a more accurate premonition, if you believe in such things.

We fortified ourselves with the cup that cheers and headed off. Jean was nervous, but this was offset by the pleasure which comes from an act of kindness. I had no such illusions, being privileged to the truth about our quarry. I was convinced that this was either going to go badly, or catastrophically. Either way it would end in tears.

As soon as the door was answered I knew which one it was going to be. It took a second for her to recognise her callers, and another for her look to change from caution to instant loathing. Her question came out in a sneer which left no room for misinterpretation: "What do you two fucking vultures want?"

Jean was completely taken aback and speechless. With my prior knowledge I was not so much shocked as repulsed. But my overriding feeling was one of pure hatred. It was a cold emotion, because it was not personal, but a reaction to the treatment of my friend. If the woman had not been so wrapped up in her selfishness even she would have been afraid. I could cheerfully have choked the life out of her.

If she had looked into my eyes, the "windows to my

soul," she would have stopped and shut the door in our faces. But she didn't, and the next words she uttered raised a spectre which had haunted me the past fewyears. I always knew that someday I may be called upon to expose myself to protect another. It seemed that moment had come.

As far as the "bitch" was concerned I had ceased to exist: Jean became the focus of her pent up rage, and the venom spewed out of her mouth. Somewhere, hidden within a flood of expletives, was the accusation of betrayal. Between all the hysterical foul language I caught the word "grass" and all became crystal clear.

Then suddenly, what had been confined to verbal abuse, accelerated towards physical, and several things happened at once. The woman moved forward across her doorstep, while Jean instinctively stepped back. To an observer it must have looked like some bizarre dance, which I now cut into. Mechanically I stepped between the couple, which brought me face to face with the would be assailant. We were evenly matched, at least in height, so she was, at last, forced to look into my eyes. I don't know what she saw there, but whatever it was, caused her to take a step back. I know what she didn't see: there was no fear or hesitation. Even more significantly this disbelief shut her mouth and stopped the flow of vitriol.

In this silence I told her, with a chilling voice I barely recognised, the truth. It is not always easy to do what is right, but, whatever regrets come later, initially it's utter relief. So, as I set the record straight: explaining that I was reviled informer, all I felt was the heady liberation of confession.

I took a stunned Jean by the elbow and propelled her back home, leaving behind another equally bewildered figure immobile in her doorway.

Once in the kitchen I sat my friend down and administered that universal remedy for every level of catastrophe – tea. Hoping that its calming benefits were not overestimated, I began my explanation. A narrative laced with liberal helpings of apology – I gave my friend the whole story. Well, everything as far as this episode was concerned. I am not sure even our staunch friendship could have withstood a full declaration of all my transgressions . As it was Jean looked at me differently now, with a hurt stare I found impossible to meet. Trust takes a long time to earn, but is lost in an instance. Would it ever be regained? I didn't think so. This truth, would remain, like the well known 'elephant in the room.' until eventually it would become too large to ignore. At that point I would be squeezed out. If my guilty conscience did not do the job first.

Of course she said she understood, but her eyes told a different tale. I had betrayed her and done so with such skill that it showed considerable practice. How else had I deceived her – the answer was plenty!

What I did know was that this was one unholy mess. I had tried to do the right, and legal, thing. Where had this led me? To all intents and purposes I had lost a good friend. For the first time I had put not only myself, but that same friend in jeopardy. I had been forced to publicly admit responsibility. But far worst than anything else – the situation was unresolved. I had left a young innocent at risk.

What could I do to remedy this? Well it would not be easy: unlike previous opponents, I had lost the advantage of surprise. Neither could I rely on the protective cloak of age or gender. I was no longer invisible.

Back home that evening I went through my choices.

Whatever else, it was a good way to postpone guilt: concentrating on something I could change. However when I looked at the problem one thing was certain, there would be no help from the authorities. My contact had made that clear. The conviction of 'Mr Big' was paramount – at any cost, and that included the safety of a young child. Besides there was no proof positive of any form of abuse. Nothing which could be taken to court or passed to the relevant protection agencies.

No, I was back on my own. I had tried one way and it hadn't worked. In fact it was such a failure that I was now in a worst position than before. Not only was my cover blown, but I had to find a solution quickly. Any moment the family would be whipped away. If the extent of their disappearance kept them safe from organised crime then I would stand no chance tracking them down.

I was up all night racking my brains for a solution. I even returned to my previous "successes" for inspiration. I thought about my Welsh experience, but a child is not a dog. I could not just dispose of its owner and find it a new home. Much as I might like to. Of course many illegal agencies do just that, but this requires an organization and planning not at my disposal.

Finally, in the early hours of the morning I reached my decision. Murder was not an option, but if I could expose the mother for the monster she was, then the law may do the rest. I was convinced they would not give sole custody to a father who was not only a known drug dealer, but on the run from his former associates. I could be wrong, but it was the best I could do in the circumstances.

So I began making my plan: trying to keep it as simple

as possible. The less complications, the less opportunity for error. It was 8.10 am when I next glanced at the clock – now I could rest. It was in the hands of Fate, I just hoped that it would not choose this moment to be fickle. Once the decision was made, my mind relaxed and I slipped into my neglected bed and slept. Nothing could be done until that evening.

Since the arrest of her husband I had noticed a marked difference in the visitors to the property. There was a lot more foot traffic: either her customers were hard up pedestrians, or they parked elsewhere to avoid the shame of discovery.

Whatever the reason, she was obviously a very popular 'lady.' Judging from the number of men in the house at any one time, she must have provided a large waiting room. This had given me further cause for concern about the child's welfare. But it had also provided the seeds for a solution, which had sprouted last night.

I had already made another call to my police contact. I knew that, despite the restraints of his job, as a father he shared the same fears as myself. He sympathized to the extent that he put me in touch with a colleague in Vice. Before we ended our conversation, and partnership, he asked that I keep his name out of it, but wished me luck. At either end of the line we simultaneously cut our connection for the last time.

My only qualm was that the incident on the doorstep had not warned her off. She was obviously desperate for funds and I hoped that necessity would override caution. Hopefully her appointments were already set for tonight and too late to cancel. Tomorrow, and another opportunity, in this instance may never come.

That night I began my final stint behind the curtains. This time I had a different name and number keyed into my mobile. The clientele began to arrive at around 9pm, and by 11pm the queue was growing. At least six men had gone in, but none had come out. I didn't want to contemplate too closely the implications, but knew it was time to act. I pressed the automatic dial function.

It must have been a quiet night. Either that or my new associate had his troops in readiness, because within a few minutes the police vehicles drew up. An assortment of plain clothed and uniformed officers piled out, among them I was relieved to see a WPC. I spared a brief thought for my poor neighbours, who would once more have to endure a restless night. I winced as the peace was broken by the sounds of shouting and doors banging. All Hell had broken loose. Some of the customers were trying to evade the embarrassment of a court appearance and media exposure by evacuating the premises from the rear. Unfortunately for them, some despicable 'grass' had advised their captors of this possibility. They were swiftly rounded up and, in various stages of undress, placed into the back of a police van. A white version of the once dark blue, or notorious Black Maria, with all its shameful associations for the occupants.

I saw all this from my perch: the remainder of the fiasco I had to find out later from my confidante at the station. Except for one incident – the main event in my agenda. About fifteen minutes after the forced entry, the figure of the policewoman could be seen exiting the front door gently cradling a small sleeping bundle. I had seen all I needed, details could wait until the morning.

Later the next day I received the anticipated 'phone call.

All had gone as planned and better than hoped. The woman was found *In flagrante delicto* not with one partner, but several spectators. There was no waiting room, more an auditorium. Obviously it was still too cold for such outdoor pursuits. Although I grew up in the sixties permissive generation I have never understood the attraction of the more bizarre sexual behaviour. 'Dogging' is one such deviation, but judging from the popularity of her services, she undoubtedly filled a niche. Certainly hers was a safer option than running willy nilly around the dark woods playing hide and seek with possible psychopaths. Did I feel guilty about destroying this valuable resource – what do you think?

The child was, thank God, found securely locked in another bedroom. Not for her own protection, but her mother's convenience: to stop her disrupting business. There was absolutely no chance that she would be returned to either of her biological parents.

Job done, but I could fairly accurately promise that I would be making no more liaisons with the authorities – that experiment was definitely over. I had managed to rescue the situation from complete disaster, but only just. It had been at the cost of my own security.

The following day the neighbourhood was buzzing with news of the scandal. The arguments were divided between those who professed complete shock, and those who "knew all along" she was a bad lot. Jean, of course, genuinely fell into the first category. Even after the doorstep altercation, her natural belief in human goodness, did not allow her to think ill of her wannabe assailant. As usual she blamed her own behaviour for the incident: thinking she had been too insensitive!

As we sat down for our afternoon tea, the main topic was the previous night's commotion. Remembering the effects of my last confession, I took a deep breath and commenced a full account, including my part in the solution. When it came to the matter of the child she had no alternative but to admit she had been completely duped by the woman. When I left my friend she appeared much happier, and relaxed. I don't know whether this was from the comfort of knowledge, or my display of honesty. Either way the elephant seemed to have shrunk back a little.

Chapter Thirteen

THE TALE END?

It's been a long journey, and life should be about progression through experience. So what had I learnt? Well not very much. I had learnt that you can only truly depend on yourself, and confirmation that the scales of justice are not fairly balanced. I had come full circle, but on the way discarded whatever trust remained.

Where do I go from here? Well I needed to get away – so I take myself off to Wales. Maybe it is the clear mountain air, but I always seem to feel better there. Perhaps it is merely that such natural grandeur reminds us how insignificant we mortals be. As I drove through the gentle undulating Monmouth hills, which transform into the Snowdonian Mountains, the first words of the 121 Psalm involuntarily come back to me: I will lift up mine eyes unto the hills, from whence cometh my help. I hope so, as I live and breath, I do hope so.

I don't know about help, but as I reached the peak of the Cader Idris Pass, and prepared to swoop down to the valley on the other side, I felt the strangest sensation. The closest I will ever come to flying, since I have no faith in any artificial airborne contraption: be it a plane or hand glider. But for those few moments I felt, as I imagine every bird feels – freedom.

I stayed in Wales for two weeks, the first to relax, the second to think. By the time I began my drive back I think I had already reached a conclusion. When I arrived home I found circumstances which confirmed that decision.

I dearly love my home, and by that I mean not only my house, but the country which formed me. At the moment though all the well known sights, sounds and smells held too many ghosts. Oh not the vengeful phantoms beloved of Shakespearian and gothic horror, but memories. Happy or sad they were both poignantly unbearable because they were the past and I could see no future. I needed to get away – a long way for a long time.

On my return I faced several changes, which appeared like kismet giving me a push in the same direction.

The first blow was the news that my dear neighbour was selling up and going to live with her daughter on the south coast. She could no longer live on her meagre pension, and decided to utilise the profits of her property, before the state did. Our relationship had changed anyway, my dishonesty had seen to that. I could not help thinking that if she knew the full extent of my deceit she would have run away much faster. As it was she had stayed for my return, for a face to face explanation. She left within the week, and the estate agents gleefully banged in the "for sale" sign almost as soon as I waved her off. Of course we made all the usual promises to keep in touch, and not to fall into the trap of forgetfulness. Neither of us believed this pledge.

Naturally we would miss each other and there was an

element of nostalgic sadness in our goodbyes, but I rather suspect that we both felt a guilty sense of relief. We had gone through so much together, yet sometimes these experiences can break as well as bond. Perhaps if she had remained we could have vanished the elephant like some magician's trick. But it is an illusion, and no amount of mirrors or other contraptions could really make it go away. My deception would still have been there – always.

Left alone with my own conscience and suspicions I wonder just how safe I am. I realise that I may still be in danger, despite the protestations of my friends in the police. Such gangs have long memories and large networks. Anyway the doubt was planted and grew. Something had changed. I realised that I was experiencing what many older people suffer: fear behind the doors of their own home.

The resolution made in Wales came back to me. I will not allow myself to become a victim, either of criminals or my own society. I have earned my retirement, and will not have that ruined by being made to feel like a worthless parasite. Perhaps it was time for that extended holiday – or should I say vacation.

The most obvious destination was an overdue visit to my American family. It had been some years since my last trip: as I said I do not like flying. The sea crossing has become prohibitively expensive since the premature retirement and exile of the iconic QE2. Such ships are no longer built they are slotted together and the modular units are all two berth staterooms (upmarket term for cabin). Yet another aggravation and penalty for the single, usually retiree, passenger, who find themselves paying a full double fare. Yes I may be taking up a double stateroom, but I only have one designated seat in the theatre, cinema or restaurant. And, try as I might, I cannot eat for two. For this one instance though I will make an exception to my "thou shalt not be ripped off" commandment.

So I make my plans and grudgingly purchase my ticket. Of course it may be safer and more profitable to lease the house, but I did not have it in my heart to subject my home to a strangers and leasing agency's dubious care. In my experience that is only marginally better than having burglars ransack the property. I mean, look what we had suffered from local rental properties. Luckily, the healthy state of my finances meant that I didn't need to compromise this option.

So I gave my house a belated spring clean, secreted the car in the garage, and handed over the keys to an old school friend. She had happily volunteered to drive over from her place in the county and keep an eye on the place. In exchange I told her she was welcome to move in if she needed a bolt hole from her family.

I kept the duplicate set of keys with me as I boarded the train to Southampton. A taxi to the ship, followed by a relatively stress free embarkation, and I boarded my home for the next seven nights. It was a full vessel, well apart from my imaginary companion, and I am always amazed at the efficiency of the port turnaround. Within a few hours something like 2,000 passengers with luggage are exchanged and the necessary fuel and groceries loaded. All done with minimum fuss: a tribute to the combined organisational skills of the ship's company and dock workers. Maybe they should be giving our political leaders a lesson in efficiency and cooperation.

I think this is one reason why there has been a renaissance in sea travel. As I said I am not a big fan of air transportation, and even less of the treatment of its patrons. Even the steerage immigrants on the old liners seem to have been treated better than most of today's economy class airline passengers. For myself, when I go on holiday I prefer to be accorded some dignity rather than herded around like slaughterhouse cattle.

The next few hours would be the only hectic moments of the voyage – until New York. I dumped my hand luggage in my room and headed up for my first meal: a buffet, the only concession to the upheaval of embarkation. That done I had time to return and unpack the delivered suitcases, before the tannoy announced emergency boat drill. A procedure generally regarded as a necessary nuisance, but approached by some with a certain nervous black humour. There is always one wit who makes some joke about cannibalism, sharks or icebergs. Not so for me: my phobia is above the ocean, not on it.

With lifeboat drill over all legal requirements were complete, at least as far as we passengers were concerned. Now it was time to unwind. It is a strange phenomena. but despite the large amount of humanity confined within a limited space, there are only certain moments when you are aware of this fact. Departure and arrival are two of them: mealtimes are another.

It was a warm evening so I knew the open decks would be crowded with the sail away parties. But the beauty of being a single traveller is that you have the best of both worlds. If you want to be sociable you can talk to anyone – at least I can. On the other hand if you prefer solitude, you can do so without being labelled a miserable old sod. In this event I chose a combination: sharing bon voyage greetings with passing fellow promenaders, while savouring all the sights and sounds of our exodus. I had left the temptation of my camera downstairs. Sometimes it is better to live the moment firsthand rather than immortalise it for others. As our last view of land for six days grew fainter, more and more of the onlookers disappeared. Many, having not eaten for a couple of hours, were lured away by the attraction of dinner. I was on late sitting, so I remained on deck as the liner traversed the Solent channel and headed out towards the Atlantic. I stayed at the rail until the English coast was barely visible. My last thought, as I finally abandoned my post, was of my friend Jean, who was somewhere out there in the evening mist. Would I ever see her, or England, again?

There is something timeless and overwhelming about the sea. Its vastness is similar to the grandeur of mountains, I reminds us of our own insignificance. This vulnerability leads us to a dependence on our sanctuary, the ship. No wonder that so many sailors have formed such a personal bond with their vessel that they have endowed 'her' with life. It is understandable – since 'she' represents a minute oasis in a vast expanse of apparent nothingness. Nowhere is this more noticeable than on the Trans Atlantic crossing.

I turned from the ever expanding view of water and went in search of my own consolation – dinner. The first meal is always, shall we say interesting. It would set the trend for whether I would spend most of the crossing in the main restaurant, or seek out the various dining alternatives.

I had chosen a table for eight. There were two advantages to this decision: the large tables are invariably window seats, and the probability that at least one of two of my seven fellow diners would prove good company. As it turned out this was a false assumption, since half of the table comprised members of the same family. Whether the two teenage girls and their mother were intelligent, or even vocal, was not immediately apparent. The husband and father ensured that no-one, least of all mere females, got a word in edgeways.

Two of the remaining seats were shortly taken by a young American couple: not all ships are floating geriatric homes. The final seat remained empty. This was no cause for concern: many people opt for buffet or stateroom service on their first night. The strain of travel, embarkation and unpacking, is often sufficient without being expected to provide, or listen to stimulating conversation. Not that our table found that a problem.

Our self appointed host was high on volume, but low on content, proofing the old adage: "empty vessels make most noise." In any group of people you always get one. I had obviously drawn the short straw. Being a keen observer of human nature it didn't matter to me: I am fascinated by such morons. Besides despite my short, stress free journey I was tired – maybe age catching up with me. This evening I was content to listen to the endless stream of waffle.

I learnt a great deal about my "host" that evening: he learnt, or cared absolutely nothing about his audience. The young couple, honeymooners, as it turned out, gave up attempts at actual conversation rather rapidly. Even my effort to coax information from them was loudly obliterated by the fog horn on other side of the table.

Perhaps they were just embarrassed, as it soon became

clear he was a fellow countryman, and the worst breed in any nationality. A complete and utter snob, devoid of any real class whatsoever. In my books they are complete opposites: class is all about thinking of others, snobbery is purely self centred. As you might expect, his monologue centred around himself and his, somewhat, blinkered beliefs. With the arrogance shown by all such bigots he assumed that either we shared his views, or we were complete idiots. As I looked at his unfortunate wife and daughters I wondered which category they fell into. Probably the one whichever made for a quiet life at any price.

I admired his family's patience, but was not sure I could take seven evenings of this aggravation. The young couple certainly couldn't: it was the last time we shared a dinner table. I did see them occasionally at breakfast or lunch time in the buffet, and we managed to get acquainted there. They were from the west coast and were returning from a European tour. Unlike their compatriot, they gave nothing but praise for their foreign adventures.

These relaxed clandestine meals continued for the first couple of days. Eventually our nemesis, having cleared out the restaurant, had tired of the sound of his own voice and sallied forth trailing his unfortunate family. He sailed through the orderly queues at the buffets leaving behind a wake of incredulity and irritation. Fortunately sound travelled faster than vision so we were able to easily evade him as we heard his approach. We said our goodbyes as quickly as possible and headed off to the safety and peace of our respective cabins.

The remainder of the trip became a gastronomic game

of hide and seek. Many people, including myself, scouted the various options before committing their bums to a seat. No doubt this farce would have been a source of amusement to the staff, if not for the fact that they suffered more than anyone else.

As experienced as they were in seeing the best and worst of human nature the restaurant staff knew from the beginning that this man spelled trouble. From the outset his demands were loud and made in an obnoxious manner. Nothing was right and everything was wrong. I contented myself by avoiding this bully all day. It was relatively easy: being a single diner I could always find a table for two hidden away in some niche.

Every night, through some sort of loyalty to the waiters, or masochistic fascination, I returned to my place in the restaurant, where it was just the five of us It was worth the discomfort to receive the wave of sympathetic looks from the adjoining tables. The eighth seat remained empty, word had no doubt got around, and the absentee had either found another table, or jumped overboard.

The gala night was memorable, and not just for the traditional lobster and baked Alaska. It seemed our host was determined to remain the centre of attention and, like a naughty child, it didn't matter if that was good or bad. The more experienced waiters took it in their stride, but one young trainee was close to tears. A mistake since bullies sense weakness and exploit it. Her colleagues and I tried to distract her tormentor and dilute the venom, but the persecution was relentless. The meal ended with his promise to make a formal complaint.

The next night, the penultimate dinner, I arrived early

with a view to giving my waitress a few kind words of support. But the girl was noticeable by her absence. Instead I spoke with her colleague, an older waiter, who explained he was also her mentor. He confided that she was currently in the ship's hospital recovering from an accident with some sleeping tablets!

That evening you could have cut the atmosphere with a knife. More, apparently, than could be achieved with the steaks, according to our bombastic spokesman. The waiters were all politeness, perhaps a little too much so. For while their words were controlled, the looks they gave were another matter. There were imaginary daggers darting at him from all directions.. A more sensitive person would have seen this hatred, but he was an oblivious self centred egotist.

The next day was the final one of the voyage, and all the passengers were busy. The whole ship transformed into a floating bee hive of activity. All the chores postponed for the past week had suddenly become desperately urgent. Consequently every launderette had its queue of washerwoman – and men – clutching their stuffed laundry bags. By the afternoon the corridors were deserted as the action moved to individual staterooms, from which grunts and groans could be heard. No, not what you are thinking: just the exertion of repacking suitcases. Why is it that the same contents can never be squeezed back into same space?

Having seen all this before, I chose this moment to deal with my own washing and found a choice of machines in the now empty launderette. I waited out the short wash cycle, and then left the clean clothes turning in the drier while I went upstairs for a leisurely tea. A very civilized institution, complete with crust less cucumber sandwiches and cream scones. It is no wonder that there is a standing joke on ships that you embark as a passenger and disembark as excess baggage. On board eating is a major occupation.

My own suitcases were packed and ready for their next journey before I made my way, for the last time, to the restaurant. The last dinner is a time when, traditionally, farewells and false promises to "keep in touch" are exchanged between the passengers. In addition this is an opportunity for the exchange of gratuities and signed menus with the crew. So I thanked my waiter, both for the memento and his hard work. As I shook his hand I tried to discretely slip two envelopes into it: one marked for himself, the other for the absent trainee. My failure at subterfuge was punished by the inevitable lecture about my naïve generosity. Americans have a reputation, deservedly or not, for being good tippers, but there exceptions to every rule. I was fairly certain that mine would be the only tip forthcoming from our table. What no one knew was that the envelope to the waitress also contained another sort of note: a glowing character reference for her employers.

We all managed to get through four courses without incident, well apart from a brief moment of excitement when a pod of dolphins was spotted. The ordeal was almost over and we were finishing dessert when our host actually did the impossible – he stopped talking. Instead strange choking sounds came from his throat as he clutched it and collapsed to the floor. He appeared to be desperately struggling for air. No one moved until a diner on a nearby table uttered those immortal words "stand back I am a doctor" and, I thought, rather half heartedly, tried to administer first aid.

It was almost a farce, except at the end their was no audience laughter or applause. Our table had become four, its self appointed leader was stretched out, speechless – and breathless – on the carpet.

Everything was done very professionally: I am sure that they have some written protocol for even this eventuality. It was all conducted so quietly: and I have to admit that the peace was such a relief. The bereaved were all ushered out and details were taken of all potential witnesses, including myself. Out of consideration for the stress of tomorrow's disembarkation we were then allowed to go. I was in no mood for celebration, however worthy the cause, so I took advantage of our release to grab an early night. After first placing my cases outside the door ready for collection, I turned in. I slept like the proverbial log. Usually the last night is anything but restful. The corridors are a chaos of noisy revellers reluctant to end their holiday, and the crew, struggling to transfer all baggage to the shore despatch areas.

The early morning tide brought us into New York with the dawn. I was up on the deck watching the sights I remembered from earlier trips. We sailed under the Verrazano-Narrows Bridge and passed Liberty Island. But, as we turned, towards the new terminal at Brooklyn, a different view of Manhattan island greeted us. The famous skyline no longer included the spectacular twin towers of the World Trade Center, A new single structure had risen on ground zero. One World Trade Center, originally planned as Freedom Tower, is still a breathtaking achievement, but for me it would always be a monument to the tragedy of 9/11. A vast cenotaph reminding us of the worst – and best – in human nature.

As the ship turned in the channel I slipped a small weighted container from my pocket and dropped into it into the depths. I felt a tinge of guilt that my first act in this new world was one of pollution, but it was too risky to take the item through immigration and customs. It had more than served its purpose. Originally I had bought with me several packets of goodies intended as cabin nibbles. Most I had eaten, but yesterday, while people dashing around on last minute errands, I had crushed the remnants into a liquid pulp.

It wasn't that there was anyway wrong with them: in fact peanuts are a very healthy product for all sorts of reasons. Unfortunately, for some people, they are also very, very deadly. I had learnt, several times, over the previous week that my belligerent table companion had several food allergies, including a severe reaction to peanuts. He embroidered this with a tedious reminiscence of a childhood near death experience when one peanut sent him into anaphylactic shock. It wasn't until the incident with the young waitress that I remembered this anecdote and my snacks.

My experience with the nurse had taught me the value of distraction. In this instance an imaginary pod of dolphins. The monotony of five days of ocean makes any deviation an attraction impossible to resist. Besides if it didn't work, nothing was risked or lost. As it turned out, the ruse worked wonderfully. Not only our group, but the adjacent tables, rushed to the large windows. Even better, so did the waiters.

Our leader, naturally, always bagged the window seat, so there was quite a crowd around him to provide cover. Dessert had just been served, so a particularly pungent and sticky pudding gave a perfect camouflage of taste and texture. It was so easy: I simply leaned over the plate and added just a teaspoon of concentrated poison.

I supposed that there would be an autopsy, which would in turn lead to some sort of enquiry. I hoped that this inquest would attribute no blame to the galley or restaurant staff. They would certainly have motive and opportunity, but so would a good many passengers and crew on that ship. Speculation and suspicion are not proof, and that was now at the bottom of the Hudson. One thing I had taken care to ensure – that the young waitress, at least, had an unshakeable alibi. I had established, before that last supper, she was recovering, but weak and still confined to sick bay. As things stood, the worst outcome would be a judgment of "death by person or person unknown." At best, a verdict of "accident by misadventure."

Somehow I had the feeling that the matter would be buried with him. His wife, the last time I saw her, was making no pretence of playing the grieving widow. She, accompanied by her daughters, were escorted off the ship, with a new spring in their step. And guess what – they could actually speak! They had all finally found their voices, and having done so were chattering away like magpies.

She may later decide to pursue some line of personal compensation. Although I rather suspected that life insurance, combined with a goodwill "no fault" offering from the cruise line would bring about a satisfactory conclusion. All in all the future looked much brighter – a truly utilitarian "the greatest good" solution. Her late husband had been weighed in the scales and found wanting: the world, at least anyone within earshot, was better off without him.

There was still the possibility that I may be called as a

witness, but they would have to find me first. Yes, I would continue my plans to visit my siblings, who were scattered across three states. After familial duties were done I had promised myself the fulfilment of a long cherished plan. A "road trip" taking in as much of the good ole U.S. of A as possible. Why not: there were no time constraints, and funds were enough for my requirements. I had long since passed the temptation to collect cheap and tacky souvenirs. There were a few people back home who would be recipients of some useful gifts, including my aunt. But those mementoes would require more thought than expense.

No, this experience would be more about learning than spending. All these thoughts passed through my mind as I stood watching the panorama that was New York City come to a halt as the ship docked. For the first time in ages I felt positive about the future, even humanity. Perhaps I was merely picking up echoes from the ghosts across the water at Ellis Island, where so many immigrants over the centuries had looked eagerly out from their temporary prison to mainland Eldorado. A few lucky ones had realised their dream, the majority just exchanged one form of servitude for another. I suspect that the successful ones were those who came with no expectations except a belief in themselves and hard work. The others brought the seeds of their disillusionment with them. Those who literally expected the reception inscribed on the pedestal supporting a nearby statue: "*Give me your tired, your poor, your huddled masses yearning to breathe free. The wretched refuse of you teaming shore. Send these, the homeless, tempest-tossed to me, I lift my lamp beside the golden door!*" (The New Colossus, Emma Lazarus)

When they passed through that door, they found no

welcome party or streets paved with gold. They failed because they expected the new world to change for them: forgetting that they first needed to change themselves. Which sort of visitor would I be? Would I be able to change?

I had not come here to work, or receive a ticatape reception. But I hoped that when I stepped ashore it would be like turning over a new leaf. A new page – the final one of this book. I don't know, I am not naïve enough to believe that desire is enough. On reflection I realised that there was yet another group of migrants: those who tried with all the best intentions but were derailed by circumstance. This was my potential pitfall: sin and evil are not confined by time or place, only by the absence of human beings.

North America is no longer an undiscovered continent, inhabited by small indigenous communities. So called heathens, who had yet to learn about the cardinal sins, yet alone practise them. What awaits me is a society every bit as corrupt as the one I have left – if not more so. The land of the almighty dollar.

Before I join the "setting myself up for failure" group, I will back track and keep an open mind. This is a holiday, and if I keep moving perhaps I can avoid the inevitable temptations. Perhaps I should unpack that camera, Focus on the beauties of the environment rather than the ugliness of man.

So I step off the gangway and finish this page. This book is closed, but will there be a sequel? Who can say, certainly not I, who have known so little of my own capabilities for so long. But of one thing I am clear: if I have a relapse then I will have to be very, very careful. One thing which this new world has, which the old one does not is the death penalty!